The Truth About Sixth Grade

**Other books by
Colleen O'Shaughnessy McKenna:**

Too Many Murphys

Fourth Grade Is a Jinx

Fifth Grade: Here Comes Trouble

Eenie, Meanie, Murphy, No!

Murphy's Island

Merry Christmas, Miss McConnell!

The Truth About Sixth Grade

Colleen O'Shaughnessy McKenna

SCHOLASTIC
HARDCOVER

Scholastic Inc.
New York

F
MCK

Dedicated to my father-in-law
Honorable J. Frank McKenna, Jr.
A man whose life reflects truth and kindness

Library of Congress Cataloging-in-Publication Data

McKenna, Colleen O'Shaughnessy.
    The truth about sixth grade / Colleen O'Shaughnessy McKenna.
    p.   cm.
    Summary: Collette finds herself unexpectedly popular when her fellow
students find out her family knows the world's most gorgeous teacher
personally.
    [1. Schools—Fiction.   2. Teachers—Fiction.]   I. Title.
PZ7.M478675Tr   1991
[Fic]—dc20   90-40561
                                                                    CIP
                                                                    AC

ISBN 0-590-44388-7

12 11 10 9 8 7 6 5 4 3 2   1 2 3 4 5 6/9

Printed in the U.S.A.   37

First Scholastic printing, April 1991

Chapter One

"I can't believe he's really our teacher!" Collette laughed. She gripped her book bag closer and sighed. "Mr. Kurtlander is as handsome as a movie star! Boy, am I glad to be back at Sacred Heart!"

Sarah and Marsha both reached out and hugged her. "So are we!"

"I told you he was gorgeous, didn't I?" giggled Sarah.

Collette grinned. "I think you mentioned it in every letter, Sarah. I can't believe we got him."

All three girls grew quiet as they looked at Mr. Kurtlander across the crowded playground. The morning sun seemed to shine directly down on his thick blond hair like a spotlight.

"Did we really get him for the whole year?" asked Collette. Even though Marsha and Sarah had both written about the handsome new sixth-grade teacher, it had still seemed too good to be true. Until now, Collette had only had nuns or married teachers at Sacred Heart Elementary.

"One of the teachers told my mom that Mr. Kurtlander may go back to school next year so he can teach college," explained Marsha. "But he will probably love us so much he'll decide to stay."

Sarah and Collette laughed. Marsha's face grew pink. "Well, he really *is* a great teacher," she said. "Even if he yells at me sometimes."

"Like every day," Sarah added.

Marsha frowned. "Well, that's only because Roger Friday gets me in so much trouble all the time. Collette, Roger is worse than ever. He should be put in a special home for the chronically rude."

Collette glanced across the playground, smiling as she spotted Roger and his friends over by the hedges. She had gone to Sacred Heart since kindergarten and it was great to see everyone again.

Collette had spent the first two quarters of sixth grade at a small school on Put-in-Bay Island, so her family could stay together while her father worked on a legal case in Port Clinton, Ohio. The island visit had been wonderful, but it felt good to be home.

Marsha dug into her book bag and handed Collette four glitter pencils, bound together with a curling red ribbon. "Here, a little welcome home present — from me, of course. Boy, was the street ever quiet without your family. I never had anyone to play with after dinner. I really missed you guys."

"Thanks." Collette took the pencils and pretended to smell them like roses. "We missed you, too. It was a long time to be away from home." She was glad that nothing had really changed since they left. The house and street looked the same, and so did Marsha and Sarah. It was great.

"Would you look at that!" exploded Marsha. She let her book bag drop to the ground and crossed her arms. "That Sherri Anders makes me so mad I could spit. I wish she'd remember that Mr. Kurtlander is *our* teacher and not hers!"

Sarah groaned. "Marsha, we don't own the man!"

"Well, he is *our* teacher, which means we own a *little* bit of him, Sarah Messland." Marsha blew her bangs up in the air. "Man, oh, man, ever since Sherri grew all those curves, she acts like she's some movie star."

Collette squinted against the sunlight, studying Sherri. She knew Sherri from past years at Sacred Heart, although she didn't know her very well since Sherri was two years older. But because Sherri was so pretty and outgoing, everyone knew who she was. This winter she did look different . . . taller, prettier, and definitely curvier.

"Sherri is always hanging all over Mr. Kurt-lander," Marsha pointed out. "My very own mother says it is not normal. My mom says it's probably because her parents got divorced last year. Mr. Kurtlander must feel sorry for her and that's why he talks to her and her friends every morning like that."

Sarah tapped Marsha on the shoulder. "You sound jealous to me, Marsha."

Marsha shook back her black hair and glared at Sarah. "I have never been jealous of anyone in my whole life, Sarah."

Collette bent down and picked up Marsha's book bag. She knew Marsha's temper had two speeds, mad and out-of-control. "I brought you each back a souvenir from Put-in-Bay," Collette said quickly. "Maybe you can come over and spend the night soon and we can have a little party. My mom can ask Gramma if the little guys can spend the night at her house."

"Great." Marsha grinned. "You know, maybe they could stay. We could play kickball."

"Well, hey, hey, hey, look who we have here!" Collette felt a hearty whack on her back. "Welcome back, Murphy."

"Oh, brother," muttered Marsha. "Get out of here, Roger Friday."

Roger reached over and patted Marsha on the cheek. "Oh, I see you've already had your morning cup of vinegar, dear."

Marsha swatted Roger's hand away. "Don't you dare touch me. I may turn to stone."

"Cement, perhaps," replied Roger, wiggling his eyebrows up and down.

Collette ducked her head down, hoping Marsha couldn't see her smile. Roger and Marsha had been at war with each other since kindergarten, but Collette thought Roger was pretty funny.

"So how was the island, Collette?" asked Roger. "I'm glad your dad's trial ended before the lake froze. My mom said you were worried the ferries would stop running before you could get your car off the island."

Marsha pushed Roger out of the way. "Hey, how does Roger know anything? Holy cow, Collette. Don't tell me you actually wrote this . . . this . . . *creature* a letter?"

Roger made a small bow. "More like a postcard, Marsha. And don't be jealous. I'm sure when you learn to read, people will write to you, too. Isn't that right, Collette?" Roger held both hands high in the air like he was waiting for applause.

Before Collette had time to answer, Marsha swung her hot pink book bag right into Roger's stomach. Roger staggered back a few steps, curled over, and dropped to the sidewalk. Collette and Sarah both tried to lift him, but couldn't budge him. He seemed glued to the walk.

"Oh, man!" groaned Roger. "What do you have in that book bag . . . bricks?"

"Honestly, Marsha," said Collette. "You didn't have to hit him. Are you okay, Roger?"

Marsha's cheeks grew redder and redder as more and more students gathered around. "Well, he doesn't have to insult me *all* the time, does he?

6

I mean, he makes a career out of making my life miserable and . . ."

"What's going on here?"

Collette felt a heavy hand on her shoulder, moving her to the side. Mr. Kurtlander bent down and helped Roger to his feet.

"Are you all right, Roger?" He studied Roger front and back as if he were searching for blood.

Roger tried to stand, his knees buckling again. "My stomach is about to remind me what I had for breakfast."

"Gross!" mumbled Marsha.

Mr. Kurtlander turned and glared at Marsha. "Were you responsible for this, Marsha?"

Marsha's face flooded red and her mouth opened and closed like a guppy's. Collette knew Marsha must feel terrible as it was, and being yelled at by someone she already had a huge crush on made it even worse. Marsha met Mr. Kurtlander's gaze for a second, then lowered her eyes. "He . . . he was bothering me again."

Roger groaned loudly. "I think I hear the drip, drip, drip of internal bleeding." Collette relaxed when she saw Roger's smirk.

"Do you want me to take you to the nurse?" Sherri Anders asked. "You look awfully pale."

Roger's eyes almost bugged out as Sherri took a step nearer. When he saw Sherri up close, his knees buckled again. He snapped them back up and drew in a deep breath. "No, I am used to injuries, what with football and lifting weights and things like that."

Sarah and Collette smiled at each other. The closer Sherri Anders got, the stronger Roger became. Now his face was as red as Marsha's.

Mr. Kurtlander put both hands on his hips and frowned. "Are you *sure* you're all right, Roger?"

Roger nodded, brushing off his pants. "Yeah. Marsha may be rude, but she isn't strong enough to knock *me* out for the count."

"That's because you *can't* count dummy," snapped Marsha.

"Marsha!" Mr. Kurtlander spun around, his voice loud and angry. "Come with me, now. I think we better continue our discussion in the office with Sister Mary Elizabeth."

Collette gasped. Marsha's temper and motor mouth had gotten her into trouble over the years, but never so seriously that she had to go to the principal's office.

Roger ran his fingers through his short spikey hair. "Hey, it's okay, Mr. Kurtlander. I mean, Marsha's rips don't even bother me, and . . ."

Mr. Kurtlander turned, his face still set in anger. "Well, they bother me. I'm not going to wait until there is a serious injury." He pointed toward the office. "Go inside and wait for me, Marsha."

Marsha yanked her book bag strap higher on her shoulder and moved slowly toward the school. Half the playground was watching.

"Are you sure you're all right, Roger?" Sherri asked sweetly.

Roger nodded, his chest swelling by the second. "Yeah . . ."

Collette was glad to hear the bell. The morning had gone from terrific to terrible in less than five minutes.

Mr. Kurtlander handed Roger his book bag and then looked over and smiled at Sarah and Collette. "Don't worry, I'll just scare her a little."

Sarah grinned back. Then she pushed Collette forward. "This is Collette Murphy. She's in our class, too."

Mr. Kurtlander broke into a big smile. "Hey, I've been waiting for you to join us." He held out his hand. "I know your dad."

9

Collette shook his hand, and smiled herself. Mr. Kurtlander knew her dad?

"Your dad and I played football at Williams together," continued Mr. Kurtlander. He motioned for everyone to start walking to the main entrance. "He was a senior the year I started. Tell your father I'll be calling him soon so we can get together."

"I'll tell him tonight!" Collette promised.

Mr. Kurtlander glanced down at his watch, tapped the crystal, and shook his head. "I'm always ten minutes late with this thing. Hurry up, guys, second bell is going to ring."

As soon as Mr. Kurtlander walked off, Sarah grabbed Collette's arm. "He's going to call your dad! Maybe he'll come over."

Collette giggled. It seemed impossible that someone as young and handsome as Mr. Kurtlander actually played football with a dad.

"Wow, that's neat about Mr. Kurtlander knowing your dad." Sherri Anders walked up and bumped her shoulder against Collette. "Hi, I'm Sherri."

"I know." Collette bit her lip as soon as she said it. That was dumb. But everyone did know Sherri

Anders. She was probably the most popular girl in the school.

"Do you think your dad has football pictures of the team?" Sherri sounded really interested.

Collette shrugged. "Maybe . . ." Her dad had played a lot of sports in high school and college. But all his trophies and pictures were packed away. He was too old to show them off anymore.

"Well, maybe I can talk to you later," said Sherri. "I'll save you a place at lunch. You're Collette, right?"

"Right."

"See you later, Collette." Sherri waved and then hurried to catch up with her friends.

Collette and Sarah stopped, watching Sherri run, her waist-length red hair flying after her like a shiny cape.

"Boy," whispered Sarah, her voice filled with awe. "You sure got a nice welcome back. Marsha brought you pencils, Mr. Kurtlander was thrilled to see you *and* knows your dad, and now the most popular girl in the school wants you to eat lunch with her."

Collette tugged on Sarah's ponytail and laughed. "With *us*, silly. You're my best friend, remember? Where I go, you go. We stick together like glue."

As soon as Collette saw Sarah's face, she knew she had said the right thing. "Come on, let's race." Both girls ran across the walk and up the steep cement steps to the school. Collette was finally starting sixth grade at Sacred Heart!

Chapter Two

Collette raced up the worn marble stairs to the sixth-, seventh-, and eighth-grade level. She had waited a long time to finally be upstairs at Sacred Heart with the older kids. She smiled as she walked past the colorful bulletin boards, filled with grown-up papers about poetry and algebra. No tiny water fountains for little first-graders up here! The whole hall looked grown up.

Collette and Sarah hurried inside and slid into their seats. They weren't side by side, but close enough.

"Where does Marsha sit, Sarah?" asked Collette. She lifted her desk top and smiled at her new books already stacked neatly inside.

"Behind you, so . . . *oh, my gosh*, here she is."

As soon as Collette saw Marsha's face, she could tell she had had a rough time in the office with Mr. Kurtlander and Sister Mary Elizabeth. Marsha's cheeks were fiery red and her eyes were glued to the floor as she followed Mr. Kurtlander into the classroom.

Collette tried smiling at her as she walked by, but Marsha was so miserable she didn't even look up.

Even Roger twisted in his seat, watching Marsha with a worried look on his face. Marsha's temper was usually quick and loud like a firecracker; she never held onto it for long. But it was still with her now. Mr. Kurtlander and Sister must have really yelled at her.

"Good morning class. I'm sure I don't have to introduce our newest student, Collette Murphy. She has finally returned from Put-in-Bay Island and we are very glad to have her back," announced Mr. Kurtlander cheerfully. "We'll ask to hear all about the island and Collette's experiences later in the day, but right now I want you to get out your science books." He sat on the edge of his desk and smiled out at the class. "We only have a couple of weeks to get ready for the Junior Science Competition I told you about. Remember, I will be judging the sixth-, seventh-, and eighth-grade projects and I want every one of you to do your best. We have a lot of talent in the sixth grade and I expect some of you to end up in Hershey for the state finals."

Collette glanced across the aisle at Sarah. What Junior Science Competition? Sacred Heart had never entered it before. She grinned. Collette loved science, especially projects. She had returned to Sacred Heart just in time.

Mr. Kurtlander stood up and pulled open his desk drawer. "Collette, here is a letter explaining the rules for the science competition."

He handed Collette the thick envelope and smiled. "The students selected as finalists from the upper level will go on to Hershey. The winners from the state finals will continue on to Washington, D.C., in the spring!"

"Make my reservation in nonsmoking, please," called out Roger. As his classmates started to laugh, he stood up and took three quick bows. "Thank you, thank you."

"Oh, drop dead," mumbled Marsha quietly from

beneath her arm. Collette turned around quickly, from Marsha to Mr. Kurtlander. But Mr. Kurtlander was smiling and shaking his head at Roger.

"My mom wanted to know if parents are allowed to come along and chaperon their kids." Lorraine bit her lip and looked worried.

"Sure," Mr. Kurtlander replied. "But the school will only pay the expenses for the student, not the parents."

Collette sat up straighter, tapping her pencil against her desk. Wow, going to Washington in the spring would be fun, especially if Sarah got picked, too. Collette waved her pencil at Sarah. Maybe they could work together on a project and end up in Washington in time to see the cherry blossoms open up.

"You may work in teams of two, or by yourself," Mr. Kurtlander explained.

"I prefer to solo, sir," announced Roger. He tapped the side of his head. "The old think tank works better with only one at the controls."

"That's because the old think tank is empty, you dope," called out Marsha.

The class started laughing so hard that Collette didn't even notice when Mr. Kurtlander left his desk. It wasn't until he was standing in front of

Marsha that Collette noticed how angry he was. "Marsha Cessano, you left Sister Mary Elizabeth's office less than ten minutes ago, promising you would refrain from bothering Roger, and now — "

Marsha leapt up from her seat. "Yeah, well, what about Roger? You *never* yell at him, always me. It's not fair. You like him better."

Collette gripped her pencil so hard she was afraid it was going to snap in two. Holy cow, not even Marsha had ever talked to a teacher like that before.

Mr. Kurtlander crossed his arms and actually smiled at Marsha. "I like you very much, Marsha. You know that. That's why this constant bickering between you and Roger has got to stop. Do you realize how often I have to stop teaching to pull you two away from each other's throats? You're in the sixth grade now, and it's time you both grew up a little."

Marsha stammered, "Yeah . . . well . . . tell that to Roger. He starts everything."

Collette felt her throat tighten. Poor Marsha. You could barely hear her. Usually Marsha talked in her loud, look-at-me voice. But this morning, words seemed to stick in her throat.

"I think you and Roger are actually a great deal

alike," said Mr. Kurtlander suddenly. He motioned for Roger to come over. "Maybe that's why you fight so much."

Marsha started to yank down on her bangs, scowling as Roger walked closer and closer. "There's not one cell in my body like Roger's."

"Well," continued Mr. Kurtlander, his smile getting bigger and bigger, "by the time you two get finished working on a science project together, the war will be over and you might actually be friends."

"What? Me . . . work . . . what?" The words erupted from Marsha like an angry volcano.

Several kids in the class started to laugh. Collette and Sarah exchanged worried looks. Mr. Kurtlander was playing with dynamite.

"Mr. Kurtlander, I think it might be better if I worked alone," Roger said quickly. "I mean, I already have a few good ideas and . . . I bet Marsha does, too, and . . ."

"Good," said Mr. Kurtlander quickly. He put one hand on Roger's shoulder and the other on Marsha's. "Share them with each other over the weekend. I want a complete outline of your proposed project Monday morning."

Marsha's face went from pink to red in less than a second.

Roger shoved both hands in his pockets and stared at the floor.

The whole classroom suddenly went absolutely still, as if turned to stone by the shocking news.

Marsha and Roger would *never* be able to work together!

Collette turned around and smiled at Marsha, trying to let her know that things weren't as bad as they seemed. At lunch she would remind Marsha how nice Roger had been to them at summer camp, and how he really could be kind of funny at times.

But Marsha's head was down, her eyes glued to the paper she was scribbling on. Her fingers were squeezing the pencil so tightly her knuckles popped up like four white rocks.

Collette leaned closer.

I hate Mr. Kurtlander! Marsha had scribbled. She underlined it five or six times before she threw the paper and the pencil back into her desk.

Collette spun around in her seat, her heart pounding the way it did when she watched a movie that was a little too scary. An hour ago

19

Marsha had had a huge crush on Mr. Kurtlander, and now she hated him. Everything seemed to run in fast gear in sixth grade.

Poor Marsha. This wasn't the way sixth grade was supposed to be. Not even for Marsha. Deep down, under all that everyone-wants-to-be-me stuff, she was a nice girl.

Collette picked up her science book and started to read. She didn't want Marsha's problems to get in the way of all the good stuff that was just waiting to happen in the sixth grade. Like entering the science contest, having a cute man for a teacher, and eating lunch with the most popular girl in the whole school. Collette looked out the window and smiled.

She was glad to be back at Sacred Heart to finish her sixth-grade year. This year was going to be different, she could feel it already.

Chapter Three

"I'm starving!" grumbled Marsha as she grabbed her lunch bag from her locker. "I never knew staying mad at someone could make you so hungry."

Collette reached out and patted Marsha on the back. "You can't *still* be mad at Mr. Kurtlander, Marsha. He was extra nice to you for the rest of the morning."

Marsha shrugged, but Collette could see the smile Marsha was trying to hide. "Yeah, well, he still hasn't canceled my working on that science project with Roger. I am planning to stay mad until he tells me I will not have to work with that . . . that Roger person."

Collette linked arms with Sarah and Marsha. "I heard Mr. Kurtlander telling you that you were probably one of the smartest girls in the whole sixth grade. He expects great things from you."

A little pink spread across Marsha's cheeks. "Well . . ."

Sarah reached over and patted Marsha on the head. "And he let you deliver the morning messages to the office, *and* be in charge of the class right before lunch when he had to go upstairs to get art supplies."

Marsha ducked her head and started laughing. "Yeah, but I still have to work with Roger. That is unfair, unusual, and utterly disgusting punishment and I think — "

Roger and Matt whizzed by. Roger reached out and grabbed Marsha's lunch bag, rolling it down the hall like a bowling ball.

"You . . . you . . ." Marsha quickly looked around the hall before she continued to hiss. "You childish brat. Why don't you go back to kindergarten where you belong?"

Roger stopped, put both hands across his heart like he had been wounded, and batted his eyes at Marsha. "We're going to have to talk about your attitude this weekend, dear."

Collette and Sarah both laughed and held on tightly to Marsha so she couldn't charge after him.

"Marsha, just ignore him," advised Sarah.

"Easy for you to say. You won't be looking at his dumb face all weekend while we try to come up with an outline for that silly science project." Marsha grabbed onto Collette's arm. "Promise me you'll come over and chaperon, Collette. You live right across the street so Mr. Kurtlander won't think we're cheating, and . . ."

Collette shook her head. "I don't know, Marsha. I think you and Roger working together is some sort of punishment and I don't want Mr. Kurtlander getting mad at *me*."

Marsha waved her away. "Oh, baloney on all that stuff. Mr. Kurtlander loves you already. He must have mentioned that he is dying to see your parents ten times. I can't believe he knew your mom before she was a mom and had all your little brothers and your little sister."

"Oh, my gosh . . ." Sarah's voice trailed off. Up ahead, waiting by the open cafeteria doors, stood Sherri Anders and two of her eighth-grade friends. They were laughing and talking with some boys and looked like they were part of a television special on being a teenager.

"Stop saying that, Ricky!" laughed Sherri. She pushed Ricky away and shoved her skinny friend in front of her.

Collette stopped, suddenly remembering that Sherri had asked to eat lunch with her. Of course that had been this morning, which now seemed a million miles away. Sherri probably had at least seven or eight people begging her to eat with them since then. Maybe Sherri had forgotten all about it.

Sarah looked across at Collette. "Do you think she still wants you to eat with her?"

Marsha stopped and grabbed onto Collette's arm. "*What?* Who's *she?* You don't mean . . . Sherri Anders asked *you* to eat lunch with her? When? . . . Where was I?" Marsha's mouth was hanging open as if Collette had just announced she had been crowned the Queen of England.

"Well . . ." Collette twisted her ring around and around her finger. Sherri had asked her, but of course, she hadn't really promised, and . . .

Marsha groaned, then looked positively mad. "Sherri is in eighth grade, Collette. Why would she want to eat with someone like *you*?"

Sarah elbowed Marsha. "I was there, Marsha. Sherri did . . . ask Collette to eat lunch with her, and . . ."

"There you are!" Sherri walked quickly toward the girls. Her long red hair swished to the left and right as she walked down the hall. "I was just about to send out the search party."

Collette felt prickles running up and down her arms. Sarah and Marsha stared first at Sherri, then at Collette. Each took a step back and watched as Sherri came up to Collette and grabbed her arm.

"Come on, Collette. I want you to meet my friends."

Collette let herself be led a few steps, then stopped. She turned around and took Sarah's hand. "Wait, I want you to meet my friends, too. This is Sarah and that's Marsha."

Sherri's gaze barely flicked over the two girls. She nodded and gave Collette's arm another tug. "Now you have to *promise* me you'll tell me all about your dad and Mr. Kurtlander playing football together."

Collette glanced over her shoulder, motioning for Sarah and Marsha to hurry up and follow.

Sherri was talking a mile a minute, not even waiting for an answer.

"My father knows three of the Steelers," Marsha called out as she hurried to catch up. "They're
real football players, and . . . I'm sure he could
use his connections to get you an autograph, probably even a real football."

Sarah and Collette caught each other's eyes and
smiled. Marsha was already walking side by side
with Sherri, bragging like her old self.

Collette walked into the noisy cafeteria and
smiled at each of the eighth-graders being intro-
duced to her. She had seen most of them in the
school lots of times over the years.

But this was the first time they had acted as if
she were important. Collette slid onto the bench
next to Sherri and put both hands on top of her
lunch bag. She was so excited and happy there
wasn't any room left to be hungry.

Everything seemed too good to be true. Collette
Murphy was sitting at the eighth-grade table with
Sarah and Marsha like this is what they did every
day of the week.

"So anyway," continued Sherri, spreading her
hands and looking up and down the table like she

was having a press conference, "my mom said that if I get at least a B on my math test today, I will be allowed to have you all over for a sleepover."

"Great!" cried Marsha. "Want me to bring some tapes? I have almost every tape in the world."

Sherri stopped, turning to stare at Marsha. "Sorry, Marcie, but . . . but this was kind of a . . . private . . ."

Collette bent her straw down, too embarrassed to even look at Marsha. Marsha was so used to being the center of attention at home, it was hard for her to ever believe someone wouldn't be including her. Sherri didn't even remember her name.

"I baby-sit Saturdays till five — so don't start too early," said the girl next to Sherri.

Sherri smiled, rubbing her hands together excitedly. "Well, my mom has to work until nine on Saturdays, so to have some *real* fun, we'll start at seven-thirty."

Everyone at the table laughed. A tall girl with glasses named Becca crumpled her lunch bag and shook her head. "My mom won't drop me off till she is sure your mom is there. I guess I'll see you guys at nine."

Sherri frowned. "Well, tell her my mom is there, dummy. I mean, we aren't in the third grade anymore."

The girls started to laugh again. Collette glanced over at Becca, who pushed her glasses up a notch and gave a worried smile back at Sherri.

The second lunch bell rang and most of the eighth-graders jumped up, grabbing their trays. "See you later," they called.

"See you later," Marsha called back. "Maybe tomorrow, okay?"

Sherri took her time putting her apple core and sandwich scraps back in her bag. "So, maybe I'll give you a call after school."

Marsha's head shot up, her mouth opened but then closed. She looked over at Collette. "Oh . . ."

Sherri ripped off a small piece of her lunch bag and pushed it toward Collette. She dug into her skirt pocket and handed her a thin purple pen. "Here, write down your phone number, Collette."

Collette took the pen, then set it down so she could wipe off her hands. She could feel Sarah and Marsha staring at her. When she picked up the pen she had to stop, since she had almost forgotten her own phone number. From the corner of her eye she could see Marsha smashing her lunch bag into a tight little ball. Sarah was getting up to leave.

Collette handed Sherri back the paper and pen and tried to act casual, as if she did this every day. As if every day the most popular girl in the eighth grade asked her for her phone number so she could call her up and try to be friends.

"Thanks," said Sherri cheerfully. She gave a small wave to Marsha and Sarah and then patted Collette on the shoulder. "See you, Collette."

"See you," Collette replied. She tried to keep her voice low so Marsha and Sarah couldn't hear how excited she really was. She didn't want to show off, especially since Sherri hadn't asked them for their phone numbers. But she would, eventually, after Collette told Sherri that Sarah had been her best friend since third grade and was a lot of fun and explained that once Marsha relaxed enough to stop bragging, she was great, too.

Collette stood up and followed Marsha and Sarah to the door. Just as they rounded the corner, Mr. Kurtlander walked in. He tossed his milk carton into the bin and held his watch to his ear. He unfastened it and rewound it, listening again before he shook his head and frowned.

"Hi, Mr. Kurtlander," said Sarah.

"Hi, girls." Mr. Kurtlander held out his watch to Collette. "Do me a favor and toss this in the trash for me, Murphy."

Collette took the watch by the leather strap. When she looked up, Mr. Kurtlander was already walking through the cafeteria, whistling and nodding to tables as he passed.

"You're not going to throw it away, are you?" asked Sarah. "Wow, I can't believe he gave you his watch."

Marsha reached out and grabbed it. "Let me have it."

"No." Collette snatched the watch back and fastened it around her wrist. "He gave it to me."

"To throw away, Collette," reminded Marsha. "He didn't give it to you to wear like some sort of engagement ring."

Sarah looked at Collette and nodded. "He might get mad if he sees you wearing it."

Collette unfastened the watch. She didn't want Mr. Kurtlander to think she had a crush on him or anything.

30

"I'll give you ten bucks for the watch," offered Marsha.

Collette laughed. "No, I like it."

"Okay, fifteen and I promise I'll never make fun of your family again," promised Marsha.

Collette bent over and fastened the watch to her ankle, pulling her white sock over it.

"We can take turns wearing it," Collette said.

Marsha tugged at her bangs. "I should get a chance to wear it Saturday since I have to look at Roger's dumb face all day."

Sarah and Collette laughed. Collette bumped against Marsha as they walked out the door. "It's a deal. All day Saturday!"

As Collette hurried up the stairs for her coat, she could feel the cool metal of the watch rubbing against her ankle. She could hardly wait to show Sherri and the other eighth-graders. It was a sixth-grade souvenir too good to keep a secret.

Chapter Four

Collette closed her eyes and leaned her head against the bus window. Marsha had been complaining the entire way home.

"Oh, sure, thanks a lot, Collette. I bet you wouldn't close your eyes and act bored if Sherri Anders was trying to tell you about her miserable day." Marsha poked Collette in the side. "Sarah and I felt positively ignored all through lunch if you want to know the truth. You spent the whole time monopolizing the conversation while we just sat there like a couple of nerds."

Collette's eyes flew open. That wasn't a bit true. Marsha had done most of the talking, and it had all been about herself.

"I tried to include you two in *everything*, Marsha. Remember how Sherri asked me where I went to camp and I told her about you and Sarah getting poison ivy? And I told her you lived right across the street from me."

Collette waited a second to let the truth soak in.

"Yes," said Marsha. "But when Sherri asked you to write down your phone number, you didn't write down all three of ours."

"Marsha, that would have been dumb. She only asked for mine. I mean, I can't act like the three of us are married."

Marsha blew her bangs up in the air and leaned back, her frown getting deeper and deeper by the minute. "I know, I guess you were trying, but gosh, Collette, I just can't understand why Sherri and her friends think *you're* so much more interesting than *me*."

Collette closed her eyes again. Marsha could be so insulting. She just couldn't understand why anyone would pick Collette when they could have picked her.

"I told Sherri all about our big summer place at Chautauqua and she acted almost mad, like I was showing off or something." Marsha tugged on her bangs. "I told her she could come up for a week in the summer if she wanted and she just ignored me. Boy, is she a hard person to impress."

Collette looked out the window to hide her grin. Marsha had pulled out her best bragging bets today at lunch, telling the eighth-graders all about her fancy house, the car phones, and her giant walk-in closet. Some of the girls had looked interested, but Sherri hadn't seemed the least bit impressed. Collette liked that about Sherri. She seemed real down-to-earth and nice.

As the bus pulled up in front of the stop, Marsha stood up, clutching her book bag and groaning. "In a few days ratty Roger will be ringing my doorbell at eleven o'clock to work on the science project. With any luck, I'll die in my sleep."

Collette followed Marsha down the aisle. "It won't be that bad. Just think of some ideas so you can write an outline."

Marsha shuddered. "I'm going to have to spray the whole house after he leaves. I'll make my mom buy paper drinking cups so we can burn them."

Collette laughed and ran across the street. She raced past her brother Jeff, grabbing his baseball

34

cap. Her good mood had been ballooning all after-noon. Sarah had been a little quiet after lunch, but she was her old self by the time school ended.

As Collette headed up the driveway, the side door opened and Stevie ran out, a cape made from a green bath towel pinned to his shoulders. "Here comes Batman, Collette. You better get far away! I'm going to make you my prisoner guy."

Collette was in such a good mood, she didn't even yell as Stevie charged into her stomach, grabbing onto her with both hands.

"I'm going to lock you up with spiders." Stevie laughed and tugged her toward the garage.

Collette broke free and ran in the side door. "You'll have to catch me first, Batman," she cried. Stevie had started kindergarten that year but he still acted like a little crazy person.

"Collette, telephone!" called Laura from the top of the stairs. "Then come up to our room cause I have the dollhouse people all set up to watch us move their furniture around, okay?"

"Okay, I'll be right up." Collette smiled. Last night Laura decided that her dollhouse people won the lottery and now they were buying new furniture for their house.

35

Collette walked into the kitchen and picked up the phone. It was probably Sarah, calling to come up with an idea for their science project. They were thinking about working together. If they spent all weekend on it, they could get it okayed on Monday and get started.

"Hi, Collette?"

"Yes?" It wasn't Sarah or Marsha.

"Hi, it's me, Sherri."

Collette broke into a wide grin. Wow, Sherri must have called as soon as she got off the bus.

"So what are you doing?" asked Sherri. Collette could hear ice cubes clattering.

"Nothing, I mean I just got home." Collette bit her lip, hoping she didn't sound too boring.

"Oh, well, me, too." Sherri laughed. "I was just about to have a Coke and watch the soaps. What about you?"

Collette glanced around the kitchen, looking down at the cookies and milk her mother had set out for a snack. Collette tapped her fingers against the phone. She couldn't tell Sherri she was about to have a cookie and maybe play with Stevie or help her little sister rearrange the dollhouse furniture. Sherri would think Collette was a big baby.

"I think Clare is going to tell David she is having an affair with Brad today," said Sherri.

"Who's Clare?" asked Collette, her face flushing at the thought of anyone having an affair.

Sherri laughed. "She's the witch on *Lives of Lies*. Do you watch that one?"

Collette took a sip of milk and nearly choked. Actually her mother wouldn't let anyone watch the soaps, including herself. At her house cartoons or Mister Rogers was the only thing turned on after school.

"Sometimes," Collette said quickly. Actually she had seen it once at Marsha's house.

"Well, I just wanted to say hi."

"Thanks," said Collette. There was a silence and Collette wondered if she should say something else, like "Thank you for letting me eat lunch with you and your friends, today" or "I'm glad you remembered to call me."

"So . . ." Sherri said at last. "Are you going to have time to look for some of those pictures of your dad and Mr. Kurtlander?"

Collette had to think for a minute to remember which pictures. "Oh, yeah, sure. I mean, I'll have to ask my dad to go up in the attic to get his old hero stuff." Collette laughed, thinking of the big box filled with trophies and ribbons her dad had won in high school and college. "Maybe he can go up in the attic on Saturday. We're still unpacking from the trip right now."

"Great. Hey, I have an idea," Sherri said quickly. "Why don't I come over Saturday afternoon and help you look? How about three-thirty? Then we can walk down to the zoo or something. I mean, if you want to — "

"Sure — great!" Collette gripped the phone and tried to keep the excitement out of her voice. She didn't want to scare Sherri off by acting too happy, like she had never had a really cool friend before.

"See you tomorrow," Sherri said. She sounded just as happy as Collette. "Maybe you can come over to my house after school tomorrow afternoon. It's pretty close."

"Sure," Collette said quickly. Actually, her mother had promised to let her start walking into Shadyside when she was older. Maybe sixth grade was old enough. "Do you mind if I bring Marsha and Sarah?" Collette drew in a deep breath, hoping that wasn't rude, but she knew her mom would never let her walk alone. Besides, Marsha and Sarah would feel really left out if they couldn't come.

Sherri was quiet for a second, then she laughed. "Sure. I'll give you directions tomorrow at lunch. Bye, Collette."

As soon as Collette hung up the phone she threw back her head and laughed. She was going to Sherri's house tomorrow, and on Saturday Sherri Anders would be walking around her very own house.

"Wow, you sound like you had a good day, kiddo," her mother said as she walked into the room. "Was everyone happy to see you?"

Collette nodded and hugged her mother. She had so much good news to tell her, she didn't even know where to start. "It was great. That was Sherri on the phone, a new friend. She wants me to walk over to her house tomorrow with Sarah and Marsha. Can I please? She is sooo nice, Mom. And guess what?" Collette slid into a chair and reached for a cookie. "Our new teacher, Mr. Kurtlander, knows Daddy. He knows you, too."

Her mother thought for a second, then smiled. "Sure, Brad Kurtlander. Gosh, it's been years."

"Well, he's going to call because he wants to

come over." Collette was happy to see her mother so glad about the news. Just wait until she got a chance to meet Sherri Anders. She would be proud that Collette was lucky enough to have such an important friend.

Collette grabbed another cookie and raced down the hall and upstairs. She would play with Laura for a little while and then go over and tell Marsha the good news. Sarah could just come home on the bus with them and they could change out of their uniforms and head on over to Sherri's. Maybe Sherri would have so much fun with them that she would ask them all to her slumber party. Collette stopped at the top of the stairs and grinned. Sixth grade was almost too good to be true.

Chapter Five

Collette couldn't believe how quickly the next day at school went. Marsha was so excited about being invited to Sherri's that she didn't have time to get in trouble with Roger, and Sarah had packed her best outfit in her gym bag to change into after school.

"We'll be over in a couple of minutes to pick you up, Marsha," Collette called as she and Sarah hopped off the bus.

"I'll be ready," Marsha shouted back. She tore across the street and raced through her front door.

"Boy, Marsha sure is happy," laughed Sarah.

Collette nodded. "Sherri is so nice. Did you notice that she saved all three of us seats at lunch, today?"

Sarah shrugged. "Yes, but she only talks to you, Collette. You must have forced her to let us come over today."

Collette laughed as she opened the door. "No way. She really likes you both."

"Maybe she'll ask us all to the slumber party." Sarah grinned. "Come on, let's get going. This is going to be fun."

By the time Collette and Sarah had changed and crossed the street, it was already three-thirty.

"Hurry up, Marsha," groaned Collette. She glanced at her watch and sighed. "It's really getting late!"

"Are you sure my sweater looks okay like this?" Marsha retied the pink sleeves around her shoulders for the fifth time. "Gosh, maybe I should change into my leather skirt!"

Collette and Sarah looked at each other, each raising an eyebrow. Marsha had made them wait an extra twenty minutes while she tried on three other outfits. She was acting as if she were going to be interviewed for a job instead of just walking over to visit with Sherri Anders.

"Come on," laughed Collette. Soon all three girls were running down the sidewalk, racing toward Shadyside.

"Here's Virginia," called out Collette. They waited till the light changed and raced across the street. The huge Victorian houses, with their fancy porches and peaked roofs, seemed almost too big for the tiny, tree-lined street.

"Which house?" asked Sarah. Sarah slid a comb from her back pocket and raked it through her hair, then shoved it out of sight.

Collette held up her wrist where she had neatly printed the house number with magic marker. "Fourteen-oh-two. I guess it's on the right side of the street. Here's twenty-three-ten."

Marsha groaned. "It's all the way down the block. Hurry up, guys, or we won't have any time to visit. My mom is picking us up at five-thirty."

Marsha marched off down the street, swinging her arms and looking to the left and right for house numbers.

"I hope Marsha calms down a little," whispered

Sarah. "Maybe we should have warned her to keep her temper in while she's at Sherri's."

Collette just smiled. Marsha was going to be so overwhelmed when she was with Sherri, she would probably just sit there and stare.

After another ten minutes, the girls were almost at the end of the street. The Victorian houses with the perfectly manicured lawns and knee-high hedges had stopped five minutes back. Now the houses, half hidden behind overgrown evergreens and wild-looking branches, were huddled more closely together, some with grassy front yards while others had gravel or nothing but hard mud.

"We can't be on Virginia anymore!" cried Marsha. She grabbed Collette's wrist and held it up. "Fourteen-oh-two . . . that crummy-looking house with the washing machine on the front porch is fourteen-oh-eight."

"There it is." Sarah pointed to a run-down red-brick duplex.

Marsha shook her head. "No way, Sherri Anders does not live in that . . . that place."

Collette rechecked the street sign. "Virginia Avenue, Marsha. Come on, it's okay. I mean, why were we all thinking Sherri lives in a mansion just because she's so perfect herself?"

44

"Yeah," agreed Sarah. "My uncle lives in a duplex like this and it's nice inside."

Marsha crossed her arms and looked disappointed as she stared at the two large trash cans in front of the cyclone fence in front. Fourteen-oh-two was painted in large yellow numbers on both of the black cans.

Collette grabbed Marsha's arm as they walked up the cement stairs. "*Don't* mention how great your house is, Marsha."

Marsha's eyes bugged out before she narrowed them to glare at Collette. "Of course I won't, Collette. You're not the only smart person in the sixth grade, you know."

Collette rang the bell, almost hopping back as the shrill blast echoed through the hall.

Within seconds, Sherri ran down the stairs and pulled open the door. Her red hair was pulled up with a bright yellow scarf that matched the yellow paint slashes scattered across her jeans.

"Wow, your jeans are cool," cried Marsha. She nearly stepped on Collette's feet as she hurried inside. "Where did you buy them? I would love a pair."

Sherri barely glanced down. "They're just regular jeans. I painted them." Sherri grinned at Collette as she pointed past her to the trash cans. "After I painted the numbers on my beautiful trash cans. Come on up."

The girls followed Sherri up the narrow staircase. At the top of the stairs, the brightly painted apartment seemed to glow. The living room was painted white with pale brown around the woodwork and ceiling. The kitchen and dining room were both painted dark blue with bright white trim. Above the sink was a giant rainbow that stretched all the way across the wall and seemed to splash right out the window.

"Holy cow!" Marsha's voice sounded so high she squeaked. "This is so cool."

Collette shot Sarah a nervous look. Marsha was pacing around the apartment, poking her head in and out of doorways like an overwound toy.

"This is great, this is so pretty," declared Marsha.

Collette looked around, liking the apartment right away. There wasn't that much furniture, but everything was neat and cheerful looking.

Sherri looked over at Marsha and then turned back to Collette and Sarah. Marsha was looking out the back window raving about how great it must be to live within walking distance of a grocery store.

"Want some iced tea or lemonade?" asked Sherri. She was sitting on the edge of the kitchen counter.

"Sure," Collette and Sarah both said at the same time.

Marsha twirled around from the window. "Want me to help, Sherri?"

"No, thanks. Want some iced tea, Marcie?"

Marsha's face fell two stories. She shook back her hair and took a deep breath. "It's Marsha . . . "

Sherri looked over at Collette and grinned. Collette almost forgot to smile back. Did Sherri really forget Marsha's name already?

Once they were all seated around the kitchen table, having iced tea and pretzels, Collette relaxed. They were laughing about the gym teacher and raving about Mr. Kurtlander.

"He is the most handsome man in the world," announced Sherri. She snapped her pretzel in two and waved one end of it at Collette. "You are so lucky that your family knows him. I bet he's going to come to your house for dinner. Then you'll be able to stare at him for *hours*."

Sarah reached across the table and patted Collette's hand. "Luckily Collette will remember her best friends and invite us, too, right?"

Everyone laughed. Sherri poured some more iced tea. "Could we, Collette? Come for dinner, I mean."

Collette thought for a minute. "Maybe, but my parents haven't asked Mr. Kurtlander yet."

Marsha leaned both arms on the table. "My parents could ask him, too, Sherri. My uncle is on the school board so he could get Mr. Kurtlander's private number."

Sherri took her glass of iced tea and walked to the sink. "Great, well, why don't we *all* ask him and then see if he comes." Sherri waved her hand around the kitchen. "I'm sure he would just *love* to come here. With any luck his car wouldn't get stolen before dessert."

The kitchen became so quiet, Collette could hear the ticking of the large teapot clock hanging above the stove. She stared down at the gray Formica tabletop, tracing her finger down a spidery crack. If she started raving about Sherri's apartment now, it would sound really fake. Collette reached down and nervously scratched her leg, almost wishing Marsha would start talking about anything, even her own fancy house. Anything to eat up the awful silence.

Collette bit her lip and scratched harder. Mr. Kurtlander's watch bumped against her ankle. Collette smiled and unfastened it, dangling it like a fish above the table.

"Sherri, look. I forgot to show this to you. It's Mr. Kurtlander's watch."

Sherri choked on her tea, covering her mouth as she spit the rest in the sink. When she turned around, wiping her face with a dish towel, she was laughing.

"It is *not!*" she insisted. "Let me see."

Collette stood up and handed Sherri the watch. She flipped it over to show Sherri the initials BJK.

Sherri looked up at Collette and shook her head. "You are amazing, Collette. How did you get this?"

Collette blushed, even though she hadn't done anything except stand in front of Mr. Kurtlander so he could hand it to her.

"He just gave it to me," Collette said simply. She didn't really have to mention that Mr. Kurtlander hadn't really given it to her to keep.

"It doesn't work," announced Marsha from the table in a jealous voice.

Sherri lay the watch across her wrist. "Who cares? It's still Mr. Kurtlander's watch."

Sherri fastened the watch and held her arm up in the air as she danced around the kitchen. She pulled Collette up and spun her around. "Mr. Kurtlander really thinks you're special. Can I wear it tomorrow?" Her cheeks were so pink and she looked so happy. Collette nodded.

"Sure. You can wear it for two days if you want."

"I get it Saturday," announced Marsha quickly.

"Thanks, Collette. You're the greatest!" Sherri reached out and gave Collette a quick hug. "Wait till my friends see this."

Collette glanced back at Sarah and Marsha. Marsha's face was red and mad looking. She picked up her glass of iced tea and drained it, crunching the ice noisily.

Sarah just scooted her pretzel back and forth across the table and looked a little worried.

"Hey, Marsha, do you want more iced tea?" laughed Sherri. She picked up Marsha's glass.

Sarah looked up at the clock and stood up. "We better go. Marsha's mother is going to be waiting outside."

50

Sherri walked them all to the door. "Thanks for coming over. See you in school tomorrow," she called from the front porch. She held up the watch and pointed to it. "Make sure you're all on time."

The girls walked up to Mrs. Cessano's white Cadillac. "Hi, girls," Mrs. Cessano said, rolling down her window and flicking the unlock button for the doors. "Gosh, I didn't even know this part of Virginia Avenue existed. It's practically in the parking lot of Food Town."

"Hi," the girls answered, scrambling into the backseat.

"Did you have fun?" asked Mrs. Cessano. She tilted her rearview mirror so she could smile back at the girls.

"Yes, it was great," Collette said.

It wasn't until the second stop sign that Collette realized she had been the only one who had bothered to answer Mrs. Cessano.

Chapter Six

"So it's definite?" asked Collette, her smile getting bigger and bigger. "Mr. Kurtlander is coming over on Saturday?"

"He'll be here around eleven-thirty and stay for lunch." Her father put down his coffee cup and grinned. "He wants to see what kind of a football team we have going in this house."

Collette groaned. "Daddy, don't organize some football game. I'll be so embarrassed."

"Who is this guy?" asked Stevie. He folded his toast in half and took one tiny bite from the center. He opened it and peered through at Collette. "Hey, look at me."

Collette pulled the toast away from Stevie and

wiped the butter off his face with her napkin. "Mr. Kurtlander is my teacher, Stevie, so you have to be really good while he's here, okay?"

Stevie pushed the napkin away. "I'm the goodest one in the whole house."

Jeff choked on his juice. "That's a joke."

Stevie grinned. "Was it funny?"

Jeff groaned and shook his head. "Boy, Collette. You're pretty brave letting your teacher come here. You *know* something is going to go wrong."

"Jeff!" Collette saw her mother frown, but then smile. "Hey, things are getting much calmer around here. I've already picked out a great chicken strata recipe from a magazine and we will all have a wonderful time."

Collette nodded. Saturday was going to be a lot of fun. She glanced at the oven clock and stood up. She could hardly wait to get to school and tell Sherri that Mr. Kurtlander was actually coming for lunch.

Collette's dad stood up and stretched. "Hard to believe I used to play football with your sixth-grade teacher, Collette."

Jeff laughed. "No way, Dad. This guy is way younger than you."

Collette's parents laughed. Collette was glad to see her dad wasn't upset. It was hard to picture him running down the field with huge shoulder pads and a little towel flapping at his waist. He looked like he had always worn a tie and carried a briefcase instead of a football.

"Give me a football!" cried Mr. Murphy suddenly. He lifted Laura up in his arms and hoisted her to his neck. "I can still run forty yards with this football any day of the week."

"Kick her in the end zone!" laughed Stevie as he hopped up from his chair and ran down the hall.

It was nice to hear everyone laughing. Collette knew Mr. Kurtlander would have a good time on Saturday.

"Hurry up, guys, or you're going to miss the bus," reminded Mrs. Murphy, holding out lunch bags.

"Collette, wait for me," Stevie yelled. He sat down hard on the floor and tugged on his other tennis shoe.

Collette held the screen door open, smiling at her parents. Stevie was probably going to make them all miss the bus, but even that didn't seem to bother her this morning. As soon as she did get to school she was going to run right up and tell Sherri and her friends that Mr. Kurtlander would be at her house for lunch on Saturday. Maybe he would still be there when Sherri arrived to help look for the football pictures.

Stevie whizzed past and Collette followed. She held her book bag closer and ran down the drive-way. She could see the large yellow bus coming up Highland already.

"Hurry up!" Marsha called from behind cupped hands. "Run faster."

Collette bent her head down and ran as fast as she could, glad that besides Marsha and her, only little kids were at her bus stop this year. It would have been awfully embarrassing to run down the sidewalk if eighth-graders were standing there watching. Collette knew she wouldn't be running if Sherri and her friends were there. She would rather miss the bus than look like a little disor-ganized kid.

Stevie waited for Collette and grinned up at her, letting her get on the bus first.

"Tell your football teacher that I want him to write his name on my bedroom wall, okay, Col-lette?"

Collette shook her head. "I don't know, Stevie."

"Please?" Stevie slid into the seat in front of Collette and dangled over, both hands clasped in prayer. "I will be so good. I won't burp the whole time he is eating lunch with us."

Marsha laughed, nudging Collette with her elbow. "So who's coming for lunch, Bert or Ernie?"

Collette shook back her hair and tried not to frown. Marsha never thought the Murphy house was exciting or fancy like hers. Usually, the only guests the Murphys had were grandparents or aunts from out of town.

"We are having a special football player guy," announced Stevie. "He's only a teacher now but he still has lots of football muscles left."

Marsha grabbed Collette's arm. "Mr. Kurtlander?"

Collette nodded, trying hard not to smile too much and look like she was showing off.

Marsha dropped Collette's arm and rolled her eyes. "Well, thanks for being such a loyal friend, Collette. Thanks a lot."

"What are you talking about?"

Marsha narrowed her eyes and glared first at Stevie, then at Collette. "How can you invite that man into your house on Saturday when you know he is responsible for making me work with Roger? While you guys are over having fun, I'll be staring at Roger Friday's dumb face."

Stevie giggled.

"It isn't funny!" snapped Marsha so loudly that Stevie's head disappeared below the seat.

"Marsha, my parents invited him, and . . ."

Marsha leaned back against her seat. She crossed her arms and stared out the window. "In times like these, a person realizes who their true, loyal friends really are."

"Marsha!" Collette laughed.

Stevie's head appeared above the back of the seat, his index finger outstretched. He licked it and held it out toward Marsha. "If you are mean to Collette, I will touch you with my poison finger."

Marsha leaned forward and swatted Stevie's hand away. "You better turn around before I report you to the office for threatening me, Stevie Murphy. They can kick you out of school for licking, you know."

Stevie's face froze in horror before it disappeared below the seat.

"You're okay, Stevie," called Collette. Marsha

must be in a terrible mood to try and scare Stevie like that. He was one of her favorite little kids.

Marsha settled back in her seat and sighed, looking sad again. "So what is your mom going to fix for lunch? Peanut butter and jelly?" A slight smile flickered on Marsha's face.

"No, something fancy," said Collette quickly. "She clipped a recipe from a very nice magazine."

Collette gripped her book bag and tried to hang on to her good mood. Saturday lunches could get pretty confusing at the Murphy house. Laura usually spilled her milk at least once, and Jeff spent most of his time picking off the lettuce, tomato, and onions from his hoagie. Stevie would try to be just like Jeff and lift his hoagie upside down and shake off everything. Collette's mom usually just stayed by the sink, eating scraps from everyone's plate as they carried them over to be rinsed.

Collette took a deep breath and blinked twice to erase the awful picture of her mother with a handful of Jeff's leftover lettuce, mouth open, all set to gobble it up. The last time Mr. Kurtlander had lunch with her parents they were probably all dressed up in a fancy restaurant without a kid in sight.

"And none of your glasses match," added Marsha. "I mean, last time I ate over, your dad was drinking milk from a Garfield glass and your mom was using a Pirates mug. The rest of you guys have to use the dinky Tupperware so they can bounce off the floor and . . ."

"Stop it, Marsha." Collette's voice was so loud it surprised even her. The top of Stevie's head appeared like a periscope, his eyes huge as he stared at both girls.

"Well . . ." huffed Marsha, flouncing back against the seat. "Excuse me if I am trying to give a little helpful advice. I mean, don't ask me why I'm even bothering since Mr. Kurtlander is a mean person and I wasn't even invited."

Collette reached out and patted Marsha's shoulder. "I know, sorry. Maybe next time."

Marsha's head hung down, her shoulders beginning to shake.

"Are you okay, Marsha?" Collette bent her head down to see Marsha's face. Things weren't so bad she had to start crying right in front of the whole bus.

Marsha looked up. She was laughing so hard there were tears in her eyes.

"Remember last Thanksgiving when Stevie hid all his G.I. Joe men inside the turkey 'cause he thought it was a cave and then shoved in all the stuffing and your mom cooked it and . . ."

Marsha started laughing again. "My mom called my grandmother long distance to tell her that one."

Collette laughed for a split second before she remembered that Marsha was making fun of her family again.

Marsha sighed and wiped her eyes with her sleeve. "And remember when Jeff got those black plastic spiders at Halloween and hid one in Laura's mashed potatoes and when she saw it peeking out she screamed and threw her spoon and it stuck on the dining room wall?"

Collette shifted in her seat, her back to Marsha. She raised her neck and tried to look as well-mannered as she could. Sure things like that happened at her house, sometimes, but Marsha made it seem like the Murphy house was straight out of cartoonland.

Marsha knocked on Collette's back. "Hello, wake up . . . Marsha to Collette, come in please."

Collette shook off Marsha's knocking and pretended she was very interested in the scenery outside the opposite window.

"Hey, Collette, I wasn't making fun of your family or anything. I was just . . . well, warning you about what could happen on Saturday."

Collette spun around so quickly, her ponytail whipped Marsha in the face. "*Warning* me? About my own family? Thanks a lot, Marsha."

Marsha rubbed her face and then grinned. "Stop making such a big deal over this. Trust me, Collette. Your family takes a little getting used to."

Collette looked back in the bus and found Laura and Jeff with their friends. Both of them were sitting there, laughing and talking with their friends and acting perfectly normal. There was nothing wrong with her family. Collette glanced down at Stevie and groaned. He was trying to color a friend's front teeth with a purple crayon.

"Stevie, stop that!"

Marsha laughed. She didn't even have to say, "See what I mean?"

"So what?" asked Collette coolly. Not everyone got to be an only child and eat in a fancy dining room every night with candles that nobody tried to blow out a hundred times during dinner.

Marsha nudged Collette and pointed to Stevie. He had a worried look on his face as he tried to erase his friend's front teeth.

"He is the cutest little kid I've ever seen," whispered Marsha.

Collette smiled back. Marsha liked her family a lot, no matter what she said.

"So, listen to this," said Marsha excitedly. "My dad got tickets for the big Pitt-Celts basketball game in a few weeks and he said I could take you and Sarah. It's on the twentieth. He is going to take us out for dinner before at this really neat place where they chop your food up right in front of you."

"Wow, that sounds great." Collette gave a happy bounce in her seat.

As soon as the bus stopped, Marsha and Collette stood up. "I'm going to hurry and go tell Sarah about the Pitt game," said Marsha.

Collette nodded. "And then I want to tell Sarah and Sherri about Mr. Kurtlander coming over for lunch."

Marsha swung her book bag up on her shoulder

and raised an eyebrow. "I wouldn't tell Sherri about Mr. Kurtlander coming over if I were you, Collette."

"Sherri likes Mr. Kurtlander. Why wouldn't I tell her?"

Collette bent down and looked out the window. Sherri and two of her friends were sitting on the wall. Mr. Kurtlander was with them. He had his arms crossed and his head back, laughing.

Marsha gave Collette her "I-can't-believe-you-are-so-dumb" look. "Because then Sherri will suddenly appear on your doorstep Saturday for lunch, that's why."

Collette frowned. "No, she wouldn't! . . ."

Marsha squeezed into the aisle in front of two first-graders, yanking Collette with her. "I talked to Sarah about this last night, Collette, so I might as well tell you."

Collette stood still in the aisle, her knees locked. What had Marsha been saying about her last night? On the way home from Sherri's, Sarah and Marsha hadn't said a word. Even when Collette had asked them if they were mad about something, they both just looked at each other first before they said a quiet, "No."

"Tell me what?" asked Collette, refusing to budge until she heard.

"Hey, move it!" shouted a fifth-grader, giving the whole line a push. "I don't see any red lights in here."

Marsha pushed Collette ahead, her mouth next to Collette's ear. "Sarah and I think you should stay away from Sherri."

"Why?" Collette came to a halt again.

Marsha gave another push, this one even harder than before.

"Because . . . well, the only reason Sherri Anders pays any attention to you at all is because your family knows Mr. Kurtlander. If he didn't know your dad, you'd still be a nobody to Sherri."

The weight of Marsha's words hit Collette from behind, knocking her so hard, she almost fell off the bus.

Chapter Seven

Collette tried hard not to look like a "nobody" as she hurried through the crowd, looking for Sarah. She'd managed to escape from Marsha and needed time to be alone to digest what she'd just heard. As soon as she talked to Sarah she would feel better. Sarah would tell her right away how she had stuck up for Collette last night on the phone.

The idea of Marsha talking about her behind her back was bad. But to say that Sherri Anders was friendly to Collette only because her dad knew Mr. Kurtlander was just plain mean.

Collette watched as three laughing boys raced up and grabbed Sherri's book bag and ran off through the crowd. Sherri and her friends took off after them.

Collette took a step closer, ready to help get the book bag back. But a tiny doubt reached up and grabbed her. What if Marsha were telling the truth?

"Collette! Hey, Collette, wake up!" Collette looked up and smiled as she watched Sarah elbow her way through the crowd, her green backpack swinging back and forth from her arm.

"Hi. Guess what? We may be going to Disney World this spring and my mom said I could ask you to come with us."

Collette reached out and grabbed Sarah's arm, both girls hopping up and down.

"That would be so much fun!" laughed Collette. Suddenly tears sprang in her eyes. How dumb could she get, listening to Marsha like she was really telling the truth? Sarah was her very best friend and would never tell anyone that Collette was a nobody.

"I'll ask my mom," promised Collette. Her parents had been talking about going to Disney World for the past two years, but every time they got ready to make a decision, Jeff would get an ear infection or Stevie would do something awful like flushing his pajamas down the toilet. Unexpected things to remind her parents that they weren't ready yet to fly four little kids down south where they would be far away from doctors and plumbers.

"Don't mention the trip to Marsha," whispered Sarah. She glanced across the playground. "My parents said it would be too expensive to ask two friends and. . . ." Sarah grinned and squeezed Collette's arm. "You are my *best* friend."

Collette squeezed back. "Sure. Marsha's parents are probably renting a jet to fly to some private island, anyway."

Both girls giggled.

Collette shifted her book bag up a little higher and drew in a deep breath. Maybe now was the time to ask Sarah about the phone conversation. Collette didn't want to stir things up, but she had to know what Sarah thought about Sherri. Some of those feelings had to leak over into how Sarah felt about Collette being included in the eighth-grade group.

"Did you have fun yesterday at Sherri's?" Collette almost shivered.

Sarah looked up at Collette, then glanced away and shrugged. "I don't know. Kinda, maybe . . . gosh, I don't know."

Collette blinked. Sarah was the most honest person in the whole world. But now she was acting like she wanted to lie, but just couldn't get it out.

"Sherri was nice to us all," reminded Collette. "Not just me."

Sarah shrugged again. "She . . ." Sarah stopped and took a deep breath. "You know how you and I clicked right away, Collette? How everything I said sounded right to you and how we both laughed over the same goofy jokes and thought the same things were pretty awful?"

Collette nodded. Of course she remembered. That was all part of the magic of friendship. You click with some people and there's no sound at all between others; no matter how hard you try to make it work.

"Well, I just think that Sherri is kind of pretending she is clicking with you, that's all."

The bitter taste of Marsha's "nobody conversation" rose up again in Collette's mouth. Maybe Sarah and Marsha decided that Collette was too boring for Sherri to click with.

"Everyone knows that Sherri has a huge crush on Mr. Kurtlander. Marsha's mom thinks Sherri must miss her dad or something and that's why . . . well, why Sherri wants to get close to you, so she can soak up all this information about Mr. Kurtlander, or maybe get a picture from your dad, and . . ." Sarah's voice trailed off as she looked up at Collette.

Collette didn't even try to hide the anger she was feeling. "So now you and Marsha, and Marsha's mother, of course, have it all figured out. Thanks, Sarah, for thinking the only reason someone as popular as Sherri is nice to me is so she can get some free information. Thanks a lot!"

Sarah looked stricken. "No, that's not what I mean. But . . . well, all Sherri talks about when she's with you is Mr. Kurtlander, and she never asks you about what movies you like or if the sixth grade is fun, or . . ."

Collette clutched her book bag to her chest and tried to look as grown up as she could. "Well, maybe that's because those questions are boring, Sarah. Those are little kid questions."

Sarah's head jerked back like she had been slapped. "Well, last year Sherri walked right past all three of us like we were nobodies. So you tell *me* what has changed so much to make her stop now."

Collette felt a sting of tears pricking her eyes. There was that word again . . . *nobody*. Sarah and Marsha probably used it a hundred times last night, and each time they were describing Collette Murphy.

"You know what, Sarah?" Collette tried to make her voice as hard as possible so it wouldn't start shaking with the tears she was holding back. "It hurt my feelings a lot when Marsha called me a nobody and said that there had to be some sneaky reason why Sherri was pretending to like me. But you just hurt them ten times more because I thought you were my best friend."

"I *am* your best friend," Sarah said quickly.

Collette swung her book bag up on her shoulder and shook back her hair. "You *used* to be, Sarah. I don't want you to waste your time being best friends with a nobody like me."

The morning bell rang out, drowning out Sarah's quick response. Collette could tell by the hurt, and then angry look in Sarah's green eyes that she didn't want to be best friends with Collette anymore, either. They may have clicked at one time, when things were less complicated. But now they were in the sixth grade and the click was gone; now it was so quiet Collette could hear her heart pounding in her ears.

Chapter Eight

Collette watched Sarah practically run across the playground. She was sorry for the words as soon as they had come out of her mouth. Sarah was *still* her best friend, and always would be. But if Collette was Sarah's best friend, then Sarah should be happy for Collette that someone as popular as Sherri was paying attention to her.

Sarah stormed up next to Marsha and they bent their heads down. In a few minutes, Marsha's head popped up. Even from across the playground, Collette could see the scowl Marsha shot her.

Oh, go ahead and talk about me some more, Collette shouted inside her head. *You two can't boss me around. I can be friends with anyone I want.*

She turned, hoping Sarah and Marsha saw how she was ignoring them both. Using her book bag as a shield, she cut through the crowd and into the noisy halls of the school. When she arrived in the classroom, Mr. Kurtlander was drawing a map of Africa on the blackboard.

"Good morning, Mr. Kurtlander." Collette put her book bag on her desk and walked to the front of the room. "Do you need any help?"

Mr. Kurtlander grinned and handed Collette the chalk. "Yes, finish the tip of Cape Horn. I have to get a few papers from the office before everyone else arrives."

Collette took the chalk and looked at the map. Mr. Kurtlander had messed a few places up, but she could fix them before he got back.

She was adding the last few touches when the second bell rang and the whole class rushed in. Marsha and Sarah walked in together, both of them staring at Collette as though she had two heads.

Collette dusted off her fingertips and replaced the social studies book on the shelf. Marsha was frowning at the map of Africa, both hands on her hips like she was in charge of everything that went up on the blackboard.

"What is *that*?" Marsha asked.

"Looks like a sketch of your face, Marsha," laughed Roger. "Your chin is a little longer though."

Collette walked right past Marsha and slipped into her seat, lifted up her desktop, and pulled out her science book and tablet.

Out of the corner of her eye, Collette could see Sarah sitting at her own desk. Her head was down, resting on her arm. She looked sad.

Collette tapped her fingers on her books, wondering if she should go over and tell Sarah she was really sorry about what she had said. Then Mr. Kurtlander walked in and closed the door, waving a handful of papers at the class.

"Sit down, quiet down kids," he called. He sat on the edge of his desk and waited until the room was quiet.

"I want to share some exciting news with you." Mr. Kurtlander smiled at the whole class.

Everyone leaned closer. Collette bit her lip. Surely Mr. Kurtlander wasn't going to tell the entire sixth grade he was eating lunch with the Murphys on Saturday.

"I just received word that there will be a fifty-dollar cash prize for each first-place award given at the science competition. I must have *at least* four finalists picked by Friday, February twentieth, so try to complete yours as quickly as possible. Remember, the oral report should be at least three minutes, but not more than five. Are there any questions?"

Lorraine waved her hand. "Mr. Kurtlander, my brother did this really gross fungus experiment a couple of years ago. Could I just use that idea? I mean, I would grow my own fungus and stuff."

Mr. Kurtlander thought for a second. "I don't mind you doing a fungus experiment, Lorraine. But why don't you come up with a different approach? Under which conditions does the fungus grow most rapidly, or which types are the heartiest? Read a few books on fungus and get some fresh ideas."

Scott raised his hand. "Do we have to do an experiment if we know now that we don't even *want* to be in the competition?"

Mr. Kurtlander grinned. "Yes, Scott. The science project and oral report will count as half of your science grade this semester."

"That's not fair!" cried Marsha. "You are forcing me to work with Roger Friday on something really important. I am much smarter than he is so he is taking advantage of my better brain."

Collette laughed with the others until she remembered she was mad at Marsha.

Roger leaned closer. "Yeah, well I've already started the outline, Marsha, and the experiment is to shine a flashlight through your ears and watch the light come out the other side. Which, I hope to prove, means you *have* no brain."

"What?" Marsha's voice squeaked.

A lot of kids started laughing. Collette bit her lip and tried hard not to smile. Roger was so funny.

"That will be enough," Mr. Kurtlander said angrily. He walked closer, putting both hands on his hips. "Once again I have to interrupt my lesson because of Marsha and Roger. Come on, guys. This fighting may have been cute in the first and second grade, but you're in sixth grade now. You're finally upstairs with the older kids and it's about time you both grew up."

Marsha's face was so red her eyes looked ready

to melt. Roger slid down deeper in his seat and jerked his head away.

The class was so quiet, Mr. Kurtlander's heels sounded like tap shoes as he walked to the blackboard and quickly printed *Science Projects*.

Beneath that he printed *Marsha Cessano* and *Roger Friday* in large block letters. He underlined their names with so much force, the chalk snapped and clattered to the ledge.

"Not only do I want your completed outline by Monday morning, Roger and Marsha, but I expect you to hand in an excellent project by the due date. You two are not going to just slide through on this one."

"That's not enough time," said Marsha. Her voice was polite but the words were as flat as a nickel.

"You may work together during recess in the classroom," replied Mr. Kurtlander. "Or you two can get together on weekends."

The whole class seemed to gasp at once. Collette watched as Roger's ears turned bright pink. Marsha glanced over at Roger and shuddered as if Mr. Kurtlander had just tossed a bucket of icy water on her.

The room was so quiet you could hear the hum of the overhead lights. Collette was sorry Mr. Kurtlander had to pick such a terrible punishment. Everyone in the school knew Marsha would rather scrub the entire church floor with a toothbrush than work side by side with Roger for a few weeks.

"When you see how great a job you can do by working together, you'll thank me," promised Mr. Kurtlander. He grinned and rubbed his hands together cheerfully. "Okay now, working as a team doesn't have to be a punishment. Who else would like to work together? Sean, what about you and Joel?"

Both boys looked at each other and nodded.

"We both wanted to work with magnets, anyway," Joel laughed.

Mr. Kurtlander printed their names under Marsha Cessano and Roger Friday. He turned and smiled. "Anyone else? Sarah, what about you and Collette?"

Collette felt a rush of happiness. Oh, thank you, Mr. Kurtlander! she wanted to stand up and shout. Thank you for giving Sarah and me a perfect way to make up and stay best friends! Collette grinned and leaned over to catch Sarah's eye, to let her know that she would love the idea, too!

Sarah was studying her hands, tapping her fingers on top of her desk. Finally she looked up and shook her head.

"I think I'll just work alone," she said softly.

Collette nearly fell out of her chair. She sat up straighter and tried not to look at anyone. Instead, she stared at the blackboard where her name should have been with Sarah's. Her chest hurt so badly she was afraid her heart had sprung a leak.

Chapter Nine

When it was finally time for lunch, Collette hurried out of her seat quickly, walking to the door before Sarah and Marsha could ignore her. She still felt bruised from Sarah's refusing to work with her on the science experiment. Sarah knew that Collette always got good marks in science, so the only reason she didn't want to work with Collette anymore must be because she didn't want her for a best friend.

Collette followed Michael and David down the hall to the cafeteria. It took so long to get a best friend and only one argument to get rid of one. It didn't seem fair. A person should be allowed to lose her temper once without a whole friendship being blown away.

"Come on, Sarah," Marsha said, walking quickly past Collette. "I am starving. My mom packed an extra cupcake — for you."

Collette turned her head and pretended she was reading the second-graders' book reports that hung on the lockers outside their classrooms.

"I liked this book becuz it was nise."

"This book reminded me of my little brother who is a big, big brat like the kid in the book."

Collette read another three, hoping that by the time she finished, Marsha and Sarah would already be down in the cafeteria.

Collette looked down the hall. It was practically empty now. Everyone was so used to Collette eating lunch with Sarah and Marsha that no one even stopped to ask her if she wanted to sit with them.

Collette sighed so deeply, it rattled the yellow paper hanging on locker 210.

"Tired already?"

Mr. Kurtlander stopped beside Collette. He was holding his red plaid thermos and a small brown bag. He held them both up to Collette and laughed. "I hope we won't be brown bagging it on Saturday. I need a home-cooked meal."

Collette broke into a smile. "Oh, good. Did my mom call you?"

Mr. Kurtlander started walking. "Your dad called me yesterday and gave me directions. He sounds fat and bald, Collette."

They both laughed. Collette felt a tiny surge of happiness again. At least she had Saturday to look forward to. After being ignored by her best friend, she would need that.

"You better catch up with the others," Mr. Kurtlander suggested as he turned into the teachers' lounge.

Collette put her hand on the banister and considered just skipping lunch. She wasn't hungry anymore and she dreaded searching for a seat. Marsha and Sarah would probably giggle and point, thinking Collette looked exactly like the last puppy left at the pet shop.

"Are you all right, Collette?"

Collette turned, looking up into the face of Sister Mary Elizabeth. Her arms were filled with yellow papers.

"Yes, Sister, I was just going down to lunch."

Sister smiled and nodded. You couldn't run to the principal and complain that you were being ignored.

Collette slid her hand down the banister and

took the stairs as quickly as she could without slipping on the worn marble. By the first landing, she could already hear the noise escaping from behind the dark double doors.

Collette pushed one door open a crack and slipped in. She kept her head down as she got into line behind some seventh-graders.

The line moved slowly but finally, Collette grabbed a damp tray, still hot from the dishwasher, and started collecting her milk and silverware. She shook her head to the spaghetti and held her tray up for Jell-O. At least that would be able to slide past the huge lump in her throat.

"Hey, you aren't on a diet, are you?"

Collette bumped forward, her Jell-O moving wildly around in its dish.

Sherri laughed and put her hand on Collette's back. "Holy cow, you sure are jumpy today."

Collette tried to smile. "I was just thinking, that's all."

Sherri stood on tiptoe and peered down the line. "Where are your two buddies?"

Collette stood up a little straighter and gave an indifferent toss of her ponytail.

"They're already eating, I guess."

Sherri watched Collette's face. "Yeah, so that's what most of us are doing here. I thought you three were glued together at the hip. Did you have a fight? I can tell that Marsha sure likes to fight. She's a wildcat. I hope she has her rabies shot."

Collette grinned. "I just stayed late to talk to Mr. Kurtlander about something." Collette put an apple on her tray, then a dish of chocolate pudding. She didn't want Sherri to think she was upset about being deserted by Sarah and Marsha.

Sherri pushed Collette past the cookie section. "Well, come on and sit at our table. I can't believe I can actually talk to you without your two bodyguards."

Collette held onto her tray as Sherri pulled her past table after table. Sherri was laughing and tugging at Collette. Over by the window, Collette could see Marsha standing up at her table, one hand on her hip and the other grabbing Sarah's sweater and pulling her up. Marsha's eyes never left Collette and Sherri.

Collette laughed. "Where are we sitting, Sherri?" she asked in a voice loud enough for a school play.

As soon as Sherri delivered Collette to her table,

she slid in beside her. Sherri cleared her throat and pounded the table twice with her fist. "Attention, I want you all to take a good look."

Heads looked up from their spaghetti and studied Collette.

"This is what Collette Murphy looks like without her two bodyguards," continued Sherri. "Those girls are like a couple of burrs on you, Collette." Everyone started to laugh and Collette hoped her cheeks weren't as red as the sauce. Even though Sarah and Marsha were ignoring her, she felt a little disloyal letting Sherri make jokes about them.

Suddenly her mouth was dry and her hands were beginning to sweat. She fumbled with her straw and hoped she wouldn't start getting all splotchy like she did when she got nervous. After all, she was just sitting with eighth-graders. It wasn't as though she was eating lunch at the White House.

Sherri pushed back her tray and put both elbows up on the table. Collette saw Mr. Kurtlander's watch fastened high on her arm, near the elbow.

"Did you hear Mr. Kurtlander is the judge for

the upper-level science projects?" asked Sherri. She pointed her finger toward Collette. "I bet you get a first place, Collette."

Another girl nudged Collette. "So what's your secret, Collette?" She picked up the end of Collette's ponytail and tugged. "Maybe it's this Rapunzel gold that is driving the guy wild."

Collette gently pulled her hair free, her cheeks blazing. She liked Mr. Kurtlander a lot, but she didn't have a crush on him or anything.

"Hey, if Collette gets a first place it's because she earned it," said Sherri angrily. "I bet you make straight A's, don't you, Collette?"

Collette felt so glad to hear someone sticking up for her, she nodded right away.

"See, so back off." The table grew quiet, everyone's eyes glued to Sherri.

Collette poked at her Jell-O, watching it dance. The silence was even worse than the teasing. She felt so guilty. The other eighth-graders probably thought Collette would be better off down with the sixth-graders so they could go back to their fun. Collette felt sad, knowing Sarah and Marsha hadn't wanted her with them, either.

"Do you want me to come earlier than three-thirty, Collette?" Sherri was smiling at her. "My mom can drop me off on her way to work."

Collette sat up straighter. "Oh, gosh, maybe three-thirty is better because Mr. Kurtlander is coming over." Everyone, especially Sherri, gasped.

"What? He's coming to your *house?*" asked Angela, her eyes huge. "That handsome person will be walking around your very own house?"

Collette started to smile. "He's coming for lunch."

Becca sighed and fanned herself. "Save the plate he ate from and I'll frame it."

Everyone laughed harder. Becca pounded the table and howled! Collette looked over her shoulder, meeting Sarah's and Marsha's puzzled stares. Collette turned back, beginning to worry. The whole cafeteria seemed to be listening.

Angela reached over and touched Collette. "Let me touch you so your good luck will rub off on me."

"It isn't me," insisted Collette, her heart pounding an extra fifty beats a minute. She was an emotional furnace about to explode. What if Mr. Kurtlander walked in and thought Collette Murphy was spreading rumors that she had a private luncheon date with him on Saturday?

Sherri held up her fork and waved it at the girls. "Settle down, girls. You don't want Collette thinking she can't trust us with a secret."

"It isn't a secret," squeaked Collette. She picked up her apple and held it tight so her hands wouldn't shake. "Mr. Kurtlander is coming to see my parents, that's all."

Angela leaned across the table and winked at Collette. "Yes, but you will be there, all dressed up. Gosh, Collette, with a little blush and mascara you could look thirteen years old."

"Oh, shut up, Angela." Sherri reached out and patted Collette's arm like Angela had been trying to bite her. "If you want Collette to tell us all about it, then act like you can be trusted."

Collette opened her mouth to tell them all that there was nothing to tell. Her mother was going to make a chicken casserole and a cake and they would all eat and talk and then Mr. Kurtlander would go home.

The lunch bell rang and everyone stood up. Angela reached over and patted Collette's shoulder. "I'm sorry if I acted like a jerk. You're okay, Collette."

Collette smiled as several girls nodded.

"Of course she's okay," said Sherri, linking arms with Collette. "That's why we want her at my party, right, girls?"

Sherri's party, the sleepover?

Just then two girls came up. One grabbed Sherri's hand. "You better get out here, Sherri. Ricky and Eben are telling everyone that you are madly in love with them!"

Sherri groaned. "I am going to kill those two. I can't stand them. Come on, guys, help me."

All the girls started talking at once, hurrying as they headed for the door.

"See you later, Collette," Sherri called over her shoulder. "I'll see you tomorrow."

Collette walked toward the garbage bins in a happy daze. She had been invited to Sherri's party. The only sixth-grader in the whole school. Collette plunked down her tray and then stopped. Her tray was in the garbage bin! With a nervous glance, Collette looked around before she pulled it out and set it on the table.

She turned and watched as Sherri and her friends linked arms and walked outside, already laughing about the boys.

Collette tried not to think about it, but she

couldn't help but remember how often she had linked arms with Sarah and Marsha and marched outside, exactly the same way.

Collette twisted the end of her ponytail around her finger and glanced out across the cafeteria. Now that Sarah wasn't her best friend anymore, things would never be exactly the same way.

Chapter Ten

For the next two days, Marsha and Sarah spent every second with each other. They kept their heads together, laughing and whispering by the lockers in the morning and hurried out of the classroom for lunch before Collette could even walk to the door. Collette pretended it didn't matter. She helped Mr. Kurtlander correct papers in the morning and was glad that Sherri and the eighth-grade girls saved her a seat each afternoon in the cafeteria.

But after lunch each day, Collette was always alone. Sherri and her friends were sucked up in a noisy whirlpool of activity the moment they hit the playground. Ricky and his friends would chase them, or rush up with a great game idea.

Collette knew she could have joined them, but she held back. She felt funny being on the eighth-grade section of the playground, like she didn't belong. Instead, she walked around watching everyone else having fun.

On the second day, when Sister Mary Elizabeth handed Collette a trash bag and asked her to please tear off the Bingo flyers from the telephone poles around the school, Collette almost thanked her. At least then she had something to do. Pulling posters off poles was better than looking like somebody nobody wanted.

Once everyone was back in the room, Mr. Kurtlander flicked on the lights. "Get out your science books, page forty-seven."

Collette got hers out, flipping through the pages until she came face to face with a large frog on page forty-seven. Behind her, she could hear Marsha clearing and reclearing her throat. She kept doing it, again and again, like she was trying to start an old car. When Collette finally twisted around, Sarah turned at the same moment and held out her hand for the white square note Marsha was passing to her.

Collette turned quickly back and studied the

frog. Marsha probably made all that racket on purpose so Collette would have to see them passing a note. The note was probably all about Collette. "Dear Sarah. Did you see Collette collecting trash at recess? What a perfect job for our former friend. I guess the eighth-graders are bored with her already. She is boring, isn't she? Ha-ha. Write back!!! Your new best friend, Marsha."

"Marsha!"

Collette jumped. She looked up as Mr. Kurtlander lowered his book and glared at Marsha. "If you and Sarah need to communicate, please do it before or after class, but not during."

Collette sighed with relief. Mr. Kurtlander was letting Marsha off easy. Teachers at Sacred Heart really didn't like note passing. They thought it was sneaky.

Mr. Kurtlander picked up a stack of papers from his desk and started passing them down each aisle. "Take this reminder about the science projects home tonight. Parents are welcome to come in to the all-purpose room any afternoon after February twentieth if they want to view the projects or to ask questions. I will post the winners by the office before the end of school on that day."

Collette put her notice neatly inside her book

and watched as Marsha crumpled up the sheet as if it were Roger himself and shoot it into her desk.

"Collette, you should ask your dad to tell you about the Science Fairs we used to have at Williams College," said Mr. Kurtlander. "The rockets some of the guys made were straight out of NASA."

Collette smiled and nodded, trying to cheer up. She would ask her dad to tell her all about it at lunch tomorrow. Phooey on Sarah and Marsha. They were doing a great job of ignoring her. They were acting like spoiled baby brats.

Collette glanced across at Sarah and caught her staring at her. Both turned away and acted like they were just looking around the room.

Collette sat up straighter and rearranged her book and pencil. Too bad she couldn't tell Sarah about being invited to Sherri's slumber party. Of course Sarah would rush to tell her new best friend, Marsha. Marsha would be jealous and then act mad to cover it up. She would probably talk Sarah into thinking that the only reason sixth-grade-Collette was invited was because her family knew Mr. Kurtlander so well.

Collette sighed and read the first five paragraphs and answered the three questions at the bottom of the page. She wondered what Sarah would end up doing for the science project. Probably something on crystals. Sarah loved crystals.

Collette pulled out her science notice and started doodling on the back. She would start her science project this weekend so she wouldn't have to rush. Collette drew a large light bulb with a big question mark above it. Sarah would probably get her mom to take her to the gem store in Shadyside to get some books on crystals. Collette drew two thin wires connecting the light bulb to a giant dry cell battery, then two more wires twisting their way to a large glass of water.

"You're not trying to electrocute yourself, are you?" laughed Mr. Kurtlander.

Collette looked up and grinned. "No, but I remember reading something about electricity being able to pass through water to another wire if salt is in the water."

Mr. Kurtlander patted her on the back. "Salt as an electrolyte. Why don't you do some research on it and do that for a project? It sounds interesting."

"Think I could make the light bulb light up?" Collette asked.

Mr. Kurtlander winked. "It could light your way

to Hershey. We can talk about it more tomorrow."

Collette could hear Marsha breathing behind her and feel Sarah's eyes from across the aisle.

"Okay, thanks." With each word Collette let her voice rise another decibel. "We can talk over lunch."

Collette watched Sarah exchange looks with Marsha. Collette wanted to stand up and tell them both that they would never know all the exciting things that happened during lunch since they were so busy ignoring her. Collette looked over at Sarah, hurt all over again that Sarah had said no to working on a project with Collette in front of the whole class.

After two quick knocks, the door flew open and Sherri Anders walked in. She smiled to the whole class as she walked right over to Mr. Kurtlander, her hair swinging from side to side. After she gave Mr. Kurtlander a note, she walked past Collette's row.

"Call me!" she mouthed silently before walking out the door.

Roger turned around and tapped his pencil on Collette's desk. "Hey, was she talking to me or you just then?"

Roger wiggled his eyebrows up and down and turned back. Collette studied the short dark hairs sticking out like tiny pins on the back of Roger's neck. He was so funny.

Actually, Roger and Marsha were *both* funny. They probably *would* have a great time working together once they got used to it. Mr. Kurtlander knew what he was doing all right. Marsha would complain, but then she would laugh about the goofy stuff Roger said to her.

Collette's pencil froze. Not that she would hear about it, of course. Nobody would bother to call Collette to laugh about it. Marsha would call Sarah and Sarah would ignore Collette.

Collette sat up straighter. If that's the way Marsha and Sarah wanted to act, then Collette wouldn't miss them a bit. Not a single, *tiny*, solitary bit.

A small white square slid across Collette's desk. She quickly covered it with her hand before she looked up. Mr. Kurtlander was bending over Michael's desk, and Sarah was smiling at Collette from across the aisle. Collette felt Marsha's pencil jabbing her in the back.

"Open it," whispered Marsha.

Collette carefully unfolded the note, her eyes glued to Mr. Kurtlander. Her heart was beating faster and faster.

Dear Collette,
 We both think you're great!!!
So hurry, don't wait...
Let's start talking again,
We're the bestest of friends!!!!!
Lots of "I'm sorry" love,

 Marsha and Sarah
 (of course!)

Collette smiled and blinked back happy tears. Sarah and Marsha were so corny. They were probably both staring at her right now, knowing she would be ready to cry.

Collette looked up, ready to smile and laugh, and let them both know she missed them, too.

"Collette!" Mr. Kurtlander's hand was outstretched, his eyes disappointed. Her face flooded red as she handed over the note. As Mr. Kurtlander walked back up to the front of the room and threw the note in the trash, Collette stole a look at Sarah. Sarah widened her eyes and grinned. Collette grinned back.

As soon as she got home she would call Sarah so they could really talk. Boy, did she have a lot to tell her!

Chapter Eleven

Collette counted out forks and knives while she listened to Marsha complain. Mr. Kurtlander was due any minute, but Marsha was so upset, Collette didn't know how to get off the phone.

"Collette, I am down on my knees, begging you," pleaded Marsha. "Please, please, please come over here and rescue me. If I have to be alone with Roger one more minute I am going to roll up and die; I just know it."

Collette rubbed her temples. Marsha was beginning to give her a headache. "I can't come right now. I'm helping my mom, but — "

"Explain to your mom that I am being held prisoner against my will," sputtered Marsha. "Oh,

I will never, *ever* forgive Mr. Kurtlander for doing this to me. I'll find a way to get even with him if it takes the rest of my life."

Collette pulled the phone away from her ear and frowned. Mr. Kurtlander was the nicest teacher in the whole school. It had been Marsha's temper that had caused all this trouble.

"My father is so excited about me entering a science contest that he set up the card table right in front of the living room window," continued Marsha, not even stopping to catch her breath. "I mean, now everyone who drives past will look in and think I am having some private, romantic lunch with Roger Friday."

"Speaking of lunch," Collette broke in, "I really have to get off the phone and help my mom get ready."

"Stop by after lunch with a calculator and some pencils," said Marsha. "People peeking in will think you're tutoring Roger and that's the only reason he is inside my house."

Collette laughed. Nothing, not even Marsha's bad morning was going to shake her out of her good mood. Today was going to be one of the best Saturdays ever. Mr. Kurtlander called again last night to talk to her parents. Everyone had such a good time laughing about the good old days.

Mr. Kurtlander would be coming over at eleven-thirty, and then Sherri Anders was coming over at three-thirty.

"Are you listening to me, Collette?" Marsha's angry voice caught and reeled Collette back into the conversation.

"Of course, Marsha. But listen, I have to go help my mom set the dining room table."

"The dining room?" Marsha sounded interested. "You guys never eat lunch in the dining room!" Marsha was quiet for a second, then she snorted.

"Oh, yeah — it's Mr. Kurtlander, isn't it?" Marsha didn't even wait for an answer. "Boy, oh, boy, Collette. That's real nice to ask him over to eat a fancy lunch in your dining room while I'm stuck over here looking at Roger Friday's dumb face."

"My dad wants to talk to him."

"Hah!" Marsha shot back. "I should send my dad over there to ask Mr. Kurtlander why he's picking on me. I bet if *my* dad had played football with Mr. Kurtlander, he wouldn't force me to work with someone as awful as Roger." Marsha stopped to catch her breath. "I don't deserve this at all!"

Collette covered her mouth and laughed. Marsha always thought she was completely innocent, no matter what.

"So when is Mr. Kurtlander coming?" asked Marsha in a wounded voice.

"Any minute, so I really have to go, Marsha." Collette hung up and looked up at the clock. Things were right on schedule. Her mother had spent the whole morning cleaning the house and fixing a huge casserole that smelled like it came from a restaurant. Collette flicked on the oven light and peeked inside. Sometimes her mother's cooking didn't work out too well, but this casserole looked exactly like the picture in the magazine. Once her mother took it out and added the parsley, it would be perfect.

Collette looked on the counter, lifting the dish towel and pot holders. Where *was* the parsley?

"Hey, look at me, Collette. I'm a football guy."

Stevie marched into the kitchen and held out both arms. He was wearing a huge football jersey and a helmet that was so big it covered his entire face.

"You look great, Stevie. Be sure and be polite when my teacher comes, okay?"

"He's not your teacher, he's Daddy's friend."

Collette lifted the helmet so Stevie could tell she was serious. "Listen, Stevie. Mr. Kurtlander is Daddy's good friend, but he's my teacher, too, okay? So you can't show off or he might think we're all rude."

Stevie nodded his head. "I'll be good."

Collette gave Stevie back his helmet and looked around the kitchen. "Mommy is trying to be a real good cook today, Stevie. Did you see what she did with the parsley?"

"Who's the parsley?"

Collette giggled. "It's kind of like a decoration. It's green and . . ."

"And it looks like grass?" added Stevie.

"Yeah, kind of. Did you see it?"

Stevie nodded, his smile bigger than ever. "I saw that old dirty grass and I threw it outside right away. Now our house looks great!"

Collette groaned. Mr. Kurtlander was due any minute. Maybe she could find some lettuce or cherries for decoration.

Laura ran into the kitchen and started to shine the table with her yellow blanket. "I have shined everything in the whole wide house. I sprinkled baby powder on our floor so it smells good."

Collette grabbed a handful of forks and walked

into the dining room. It was great the way the whole family was excited about Mr. Kurtlander coming over. It was like a giant party. They were glad to be back home in their own house, ready to welcome back old friends.

Collette smiled. She was excited about Sherri Anders coming. Collette felt her cheeks grow warm, wondering when she would ever think of Sherri Anders as just "Sherri."

"The table looks great, Collette," her mother said as she hurried into the dining room. She ran her fingers through her dark hair and sighed. "Gosh, I wish *I* looked great — I look old."

"You *do* look great, Mom." Collette hugged her as she walked into the kitchen.

Collette turned as her father walked in, carrying a huge box of his old sports stuff from the attic. He had a purple Williams baseball cap on his head and a silly-looking grin on his face. He had been acting kind of strange all morning, like he was going to a party.

"I can't believe it's been so long," sighed Mrs. Murphy. "Brad probably won't recognize me."

"Doorbell!" cried Stevie, racing through the room.

Collette nearly dropped the forks as her father

turned and grabbed her mother, picking her up, and spinning her around. "You haven't changed a bit. Look, I can still lift what I married. Come on, I bet that's Brad now!"

Collette laughed. Her parents were so goofy, especially when they were in a good mood.

As soon as Mr. Kurtlander walked in, the fun began and everyone started talking and laughing. Laura kept passing a bowl of peanuts around and around. Jeff asked a million questions about football and professional league averages. Collette hid in the dining room until her parents stopped pounding Mr. Kurtlander on the back and hugging him.

"I can't believe you two have four children," laughed Mr. Kurtlander. "Kate, you still look twenty-two."

From the dining room, Collette grinned as her mother's face went red.

"I can't believe how time has passed so quickly. I think the last time we saw you was seven years ago at your wed — " Mrs. Murphy's face went from red to scarlet.

Mr. Kurtlander nodded his head. "My wedding. Well, things didn't work out. Carrie's remarried.

In fact," Mr. Kurtlander pulled out a picture, "let me give you her number on the back of this team picture." He held it up and smiled at Collette's dad. "Remember the day we beat Amherst, twenty-eight–ten?"

Mr. Kurtlander bent and scribbled Carrie's number. "Call her. She would love to hear from you."

Collette took a step back. Mr. Kurtlander had been married before! And then something happened and now his wife was married to somebody else. Collette glanced over her shoulder at the phone in the kitchen. Wow, wait till Sarah heard about this.

"I'm sorry," Collette's mother was saying in a low voice.

Mr. Kurtlander held up his hands. "Nobody's fault."

"Of course," Mrs. Murphy said quickly.

There was a silence, then everyone started talking at once, a little too loud and too fast, like the sound had been flicked on in a hurry.

Collette gripped the vegetable-and-dip platter and hurried in. She felt a little funny, seeing Mr. Kurtlander again. After he had taken the note from her, she tried not to look him right in the eye. Now she *had* to look at him.

"Well, hello there," said Mr. Kurtlander cheerfully. He smiled at Collette. He was probably over being mad about the note.

"Hi, Mr. Kurtlander," said Collette. "Do you want some note — I mean dip?"

Mr. Kurtlander laughed so hard he had to get out his handkerchief and wipe his eyes. Collette finally laughed, but not too hard. Her parents were smiling to be polite, but you could tell that they didn't get the joke.

Stevie clomped into the room, his football helmet wiggling to the left and right.

"Boy, you didn't tell me a real football player would be here," said Mr. Kurtlander. "What position do you play?"

Stevie stood up straighter and put his hands on his hips. "I'm a quarterback named Stevie."

"Hi, Stevie. I'm Mr. Kurtlander."

Collette was proud of Stevie for shaking hands so nicely.

Soon everyone was talking and laughing. It was like a real party. Jeff got everyone some iced tea, and Stevie only spilled half of his. Collette blotted it up before it got anywhere near Mr. Kurtlander's shoes. Collette sat back on the couch, almost wishing Marsha were here to see how perfect the whole morning was going.

Stevie took off his helmet and sat next to Mr. Kurtlander, staring up at him like he was a real football player.

When the oven buzzer went off, Mrs. Murphy looked over at Collette and motioned her to the kitchen.

Collette nodded and got up, proud to be in charge of the chicken casserole.

While she was in the kitchen, poking the center of the casserole with a fork, she heard a tapping at the window.

Marsha's face was smashed against the windowpane. Even flattened, she looked ready to explode.

"I couldn't stand it over there another moment," Marsha announced as she hurried in the back door. She slumped into a chair and frowned. "Roger is sitting over there asking me all sorts of personal and very private questions. . . ."

"Like what?"

"Like what I want to do for a science project,

like if I think magnetic properties are important, and if I could make stalactites out of clay . . . boy, he can be so annoying."

Collette smiled. "Marsha, he *has* to ask you those questions. That's why he's in your living room."

Marsha slid into a kitchen chair. "He's in my living room because Mr. Kurtlander hates me."

Collette took a step closer and clamped a hand over Marsha's mouth. "Shush! Mr. Kurtlander is in *my* living room right now, Marsha."

Marsha slapped her hand to her forehead. "Boy, oh, boy. You get caught reading a note and the man comes here for lunch. I say one tiny thing to Roger Friday and I'm sentenced to weeks of punishment."

Collette grinned. "You and Roger have been fighting for years."

Marsha grinned. "Yeah, and trust me, after this morning, I am definitely winning. I went in the kitchen and put salt in his iced tea and he is too stubborn to admit I did it. He keeps sipping it and saying, 'Yummy.' "

She stood up and walked closer to the casserole. "Boy, does that smell good. Can I have a bite?"

She picked up a fork and let it hover above the steaming dish.

"No, this is for lunch." Collette pushed Marsha's fork away. "My mom made it. Doesn't it look great?"

Marsha crossed her arms and frowned. "My mother made a quiche and she actually asked Roger to stay for lunch. Boy, if this ever leaks out, I'm quitting school. If Roger tries to hold my chair I'll floor him."

Collette handed Marsha back her fork. Poor Marsha. She looked positively miserable. "Just take one little bite."

Marsha blew on the steaming fork and popped it in her mouth. "Yummy," she said and then laughed.

Collette patted down the hole Marsha created and then added some twisted lemon rinds. She added a cherry and sprinkled on some paprika. At least it didn't look so white.

"Why don't you just use parsley like other people?" asked Marsha. "Your casserole is starting to look like a float in a parade."

Collette put down an orange slice and frowned at Marsha. "Go home and eat your quiche."

111

Marsha let her fork clatter in the sink and wiped her hands on her jeans. "Tell Mr. Kurtlander that I am very upset and I will never, ever, forgive him for the rest of my life."

Collette grinned. "I'll do that, Marsha. As soon as we sit down. Bye!"

Marsha gave a sad little wave and headed for the back door.

Collette slid her hands into the pot holders. The casserole looked great, the warm rolls smelled good and —

"Holy cow, watch where you're going, Marcie!"

Collette set the casserole down and hurried to the back door. Sherri was brushing off her shoulder while Marsha stood staring with her mouth open.

Collette glanced up at the wall clock. It was only twelve-fifteen. Sherri was over three hours early!

Sherri shook back her red hair and pushed up both sleeves of her pale blue sweater. "Gosh, you nearly knocked me over. You must be in a real hurry to get home."

Marsha barely nodded, her eyes moving from Sherri's cropped knit sweater to the tight black jeans that seemed to flow right into her white leather cowboy boots.

Collette pulled Marsha aside. "Come on in, Sherri."

"Thanks." As she passed, a wave of perfume looped around both Collette and Marsha.

"Boy, do you look pretty," whispered Marsha. "You look exactly like the girl on *Lives of Lies*."

Sherri grinned. "Thanks. I love that show."

Collette picked up her pot holders again. Sherri looked almost twenty-five with the jeans and her hair pulled back that way. Boy, Sacred Heart uniforms sure made everyone look alike in school.

"Sorry I'm early but my mom had to go into work at noon, so . . ." Sherri shrugged. Then she looked down at the casserole. "Oh, geez, you guys didn't eat yet?"

Marsha nodded. "Mr. Kurtlander is in there."

Sherri bit her lip and grinned. "What's he wearing?"

Collette shook her head. "Sherri, let me take this in and then we can go upstairs. I'm not really hungry, and — "

Sherri stopped Collette, her long pink nails digging into her arm. "Oh, I feel *soooooo* bad. I knew

113

I should have called first. I don't want to be in the way. Here, let me just take a walk and come back in an hour."

Collette's cheeks were so hot she almost put the pot holders next to them. Any minute now Sherri was going to fly out of her kitchen, feeling terrible, and it would all be Collette's fault.

"You could come to my house," Marsha offered.

Sherri headed toward the back door. "No, I feel terrible. I'll just wait outside and — "

"Sherri, wait!" Collette rushed forward. "Hey, my mom won't care if you stay." She pointed to the casserole. "Look, we have enough to feed an army."

Sherri paused. "Gosh, I feel so rude. Are you sure?"

Collette nodded. "Positive. Now we will have even more time to do everything we planned."

Marsha looked up, a small frown beginning.

Sherri laughed. "Great! After lunch we can look for the football pictures, and then take a walk and . . ." Sherri picked up a handful of Collette's thick blonde hair. "I would love to teach you how to French braid. You would look so cool."

Collette smiled. "Sounds great."

114

"Maybe I could come back and watch," said Marsha.

"Sure! Try to hurry, Marsha," said Collette. She was so excited and happy she wanted to share it with everyone.

Sherri turned and pulled Collette down the hall toward the laughter coming from the living room. "Now, let me know if your mom minds . . ."

Collette shook her head. Her mother wouldn't mind. She would probably be thrilled to finally meet the most popular girl at Sacred Heart, and proud her daughter was lucky enough to be picked for her friend.

Chapter Twelve

Collette pushed her carrot cake away. She wasn't very hungry. Too much of her was disappointed. Saturday was not turning out to be that much fun after all.

Sherri never did leave the dining room. She was nice to everyone, but talked a mile a minute to Mr. Kurtlander. She told him all about her plans for her science experiment and asked dozens and dozens of questions.

Collette reached up and felt her ponytail. No French braid. Every time Collette suggested that they finish dessert and go upstairs, Sherri would shake her head and ask Mr. Kurtlander another question.

116

"Sherri, you look just like Collette's Barbie dolls," declared Stevie. He pointed a stubby finger toward Sherri's eyes. "Especially you look like her rock star Barbie!"

Collette choked on her milk while everyone else laughed. She grabbed for her napkin and nearly inhaled it. Honestly!

"Stevie, I don't play with Barbies," sputtered Collette.

"Yes, you do, Collette," Laura reminded her sweetly. " 'Member last night when you helped me set up their wedding?"

Everyone laughed again. Collette started to shred her napkin in her lap. All week she had been looking forward to this day and now it turned out to be a fizzle.

"You look just like a Steeler football player to me, Stevie," said Sherri. She tapped a perfect pink nail on his little arm. "That quarterback with all the muscles."

Stevie sat up straighter and wiped the milk from his mouth. "I am so strong. Try and push me off this chair, Sherri."

"Stevie!" Collette hissed. "Come on, Sherri. Let's go upstairs. Mom, may we be excused?"

"Sure, thanks for the help." Mrs. Murphy reached for Mr. Kurtlander's cup. "Brad, would you like some more coffee?"

Mr. Kurtlander shook his head. "No, thank you. Lunch was delicious! I hate to eat and run but I'm moving to a larger apartment this afternoon and I still need a few more boxes."

Collette smiled. She liked having Mr. Kurtlander around. He was funny and nice to everyone. But maybe if he left Sherri would want to go upstairs to talk and act more like a friend. She hadn't even seen Collette's bedroom yet.

Everyone got up from the table, thanking each other and laughing again. "Next time I'll grill some hot dogs," promised Mr. Kurtlander.

"I really should be going, too," Sherri said. She held out her thumb like she was hitchhiking. "Could you drop me off in Shadyside, Mr. Kurtlander?"

"What?" Collette nearly dropped the plates she was stacking. "Sherri, you can't leave now — I thought we were going to go upstairs, and then to the zoo and . . ."

Sherri sighed and shook her head. "I am too excited about the science experiment. I have to

118

pick up some plants at the nursery and then I want to just get going on it."

Mr. Kurtlander nodded. "Those outlines have to be in by Friday."

Collette couldn't believe Sherri was leaving. She hadn't left Mr. Kurtlander's side during the whole visit. Collette frowned as Mr. Kurtlander and Sherri thanked everyone and then ran down to his car and got in. Mr. Kurtlander held Sherri's door while she laughed and thanked him a hundred times, as if he had just thrown his coat over a puddle for her.

Collette's mother joined her next to the window. "What grade is Sherri in?" she asked.

"Eighth," said Collette. She turned and smiled at her mother. "Isn't she pretty?"

Mrs. Murphy's eyes widened, but she nodded. "Yes. Very grown up. Gosh, I never looked like that in the eighth grade." She put her arm around Collette and gave her a squeeze. "I'm not sure I *ever* looked like that."

Collette studied her mother's face. It was hard to tell when her mother's jokes were serious. "You like her though, don't you? I mean, she can't help it she's so pretty and . . . and — "

"And has such a nice figure?" her mother finished. She let the curtain fall back and smiled. "No, but that sweater was a little tight, honey. And the eye shadow was — "

"Mom!" Collette's voice surprised herself. It was near tears. "You sound like Marsha. Marsha is so jealous that — "

Mrs. Murphy's smile disappeared. "I am certainly *not* jealous of Sherri Anders, Collette. You watch your tone of voice with me. Sherri seems like a nice girl, but she seems a little too sophisticated and — "

Collette slumped against the couch. "Too sophisticated for an ordinary, boring sixth-grader like me, you mean."

Her mother smiled, pushing back Collette's hair. "Honey, you are not boring. You are beautiful and sweet. I don't want you to ever change."

Collette refused to smile back. At the rate she was going, she never *would* change. She would never ever be able to look like Sherri, not in a million years.

"Mom, Sherri is usually . . . well, quieter and . . ." Collette stopped. Today really shouldn't have counted. The next time Sherri came over, Collette would make sure no other company was there. Then her mother would realize that having someone as popular and pretty as Sherri Anders for a friend was the best thing that could happen to a girl. Especially an ordinary sixth-grader like Collette.

Chapter Thirteen

On Monday morning, Mr. Kurtlander was so excited about the work Roger and Marsha had done together, he clapped.

"This is wonderful," announced Mr. Kurtlander. "I knew if you two worked together, instead of against each other, you'd make real progress. Your idea of a slide show while you give the oral report is terrific."

Marsha grinned and nodded her head as if she totally agreed with Mr. Kurtlander. Roger just scratched the back of his head and looked relieved.

"I'm sure the judges at Hershey will be equally impressed," continued Mr. Kurtlander. "Are you going to make the stalactites and stalagmites from clay or plaster of paris?"

"What judges?" Marsha and Roger asked together.

Mr. Kurtlander grinned like he was about to hand out Christmas presents. "If your finished project is half as good as your outline and ideas, you'll go on to Hershey and possibly to Washington in the spring!"

Marsha's mouth and eyes opened to their widest. "No *way!*"

Mr. Kurtlander's smile grew smaller.

"You said we only had to work on *this* dumb project together, Mr. Kurtlander. And the only reason we did so much more was so you would let us go out at recess." She shoved her fist through her bangs. "You never once said that we were going . . . going on tour together. You never even hinted that I would be forced to work for one more minute with Roger. It isn't fair!"

Mr. Kurtlander's hand shot up like a red flag. "Enough said. I think it is important for you both to see this through."

Collette bit into her pencil. You could tell Mr. Kurtlander was new to Sacred Heart. All the other teachers, even the janitors, knew that it was dangerous to keep Marsha and Roger together too much.

"You'll do fine," reassured Mr. Kurtlander. He smiled down at the outline again.

"Fine?" asked Marsha, her voice cracking. Collette leaned forward in her seat, wishing she could raise her hand and tell Mr. Kurtlander that Marsha had suffered enough.

Collette had never seen Marsha this upset before. Her face was blotchy, her bangs had been shoved up, and now she was chewing her thumbnail. Any minute now she was going to burst into tears.

Roger had been shifting from one foot to the next ever since Mr. Kurtlander had suggested he continue to work with Marsha. "Maybe Marsha should just work alone or with Collette on this," suggested Roger. "I mean, they live right across the street from each other and . . . and they are friends, and . . ."

"Are these ideas half yours, Roger?" Mr. Kurtlander asked quietly. "Or did Marsha do all of the work?"

Roger's face flooded red, his ears seemed to

124

swell. "No way, I worked all afternoon on that. I'm the one who took it home to type!"

Mr. Kurtlander stood up and handed Roger the outline. "Exactly — I'm sure you both worked hard. If you keep up the good work, I am betting you'll both go to Washington, D.C., for the finals."

Marsha rolled her eyes up to the ceiling like that was the last thing she wanted to do in the world.

"I'll be glad to help you both in any way that I can," Mr. Kurtlander said finally. He stood up and closed the classroom door, his way of saying the discussion was closed as well.

Collette watched as Marsha and Roger walked slowly back to their seats. Mr. Kurtlander's offer of help wasn't enough. Roger and Marsha were allergic to each other, always making each other miserable.

Roger slid into his seat, snapping his yellow pencil in half.

The rest of the morning seemed pretty dull. Mr. Kurtlander taught the same subjects, hands were still raised and questions answered. But the zip seemed to have been zapped from the class. Marsha and Roger didn't raise their hands at all. In the middle of math, when the pencil sharpener fell off and spattered shavings all over the floor, a few kids laughed, but Roger didn't hop up and run out of the room to get the janitor, or make a funny crack the way he normally would. He just sat at his desk, tapping his pencil and looking miserable.

Collette glanced over at Marsha. She was bent over her desk, scribbling spiders spinning webs around a large fly. Roger was the fly.

In the middle of reading, Sherri Anders gave two quick knocks at the door and walked in. She smiled out at the class as she passed in front of them. Collette sat up straighter, wondering if she should give a small wave. It amazed Collette that Sherri didn't seem the least bit nervous about interrupting a class. She walked right up to Mr. Kurtlander at the blackboard, smiling at him as if he had been waiting all morning for these papers.

"Thank you, Sherri," said Mr. Kurtlander, placing the papers in his center desk drawer.

"You're welcome, Mr. Kurtlander," Sherri said and laughed. As she passed by Collette's row, she slowed and mouthed the words, "See you at lunch, Collette!"

"All right now." Mr. Kurtlander tossed the chalk back on the ledge and rubbed his hands together. "Is anyone interested in watching the rest of *The Watcher in the Woods* before lunch?"

"No," mumbled Marsha from her desk. It was loud enough for most of the class to hear, but low enough for Mr. Kurtlander to ignore.

He glanced from Marsha to Roger, then pushed the VCR into place. Collette could tell Mr. Kurtlander was upset. He looked like teaching sixth grade was beginning to wear him out more than football used to.

Collette was glad when the screen lit up and the lights went out. You couldn't tell who was frowning and mad that Mr. Kurtlander was forcing Marsha and Roger to work together. Collette slid down in her seat, her eyes on the screen ahead, her mind busy flipping through everything that had already happened since she had returned to Sacred Heart. Being upstairs with the older kids meant harder classes, more responsibility, and a lot more confusion. Too bad sixth grade didn't come with a set of directions!

Chapter Fourteen

Every day for the next few weeks, more and more science projects were brought in and displayed in the all-purpose room. Mr. Kurtlander was his old cheerful self, glad that everyone was taking the science competition so seriously.

"I am so impressed," commented Mr. Kurtlander as he walked up and down the aisles, examining the new projects. "I can hardly wait to see what will come in tomorrow."

Collette hurried with Marsha to the bus. She would have to finish hers tonight. So far she hadn't had too much time to work on the project. She had her light bulb attached to the dry cell and it did light up when she added salt to the water, but it looked so boring. Collette would have to really spend some time on dressing it up a little.

"My mom will drive us to school when we bring in our projects," promised Marsha. "Gosh, my prison sentence is almost over. In a few more days Roger Friday will never have to step foot in my house again."

"Oh, it hasn't been so bad, Marsha," giggled Collette. "Roger is funny."

Marsha broke into a grin. "I know. The other night Roger made little stalactite teeth and wore them. He pretended he was a little cave bat and he wanted to drain my blood. He is so weird!"

Collette leaned back in her seat, glad that things were finally calming down in the sixth grade.

"My dad wants to leave around five-thirty on Friday so we won't have to rush through dinner," explained Marsha. "We are going to have so much fun. Sarah is allowed to spend the night so ask your mom if you can, too."

Collette gripped her book bag and turned to Marsha. "What? You don't mean *this* Friday, do you?"

Marsha grinned. "Yes, Collette. My dad already bought the tickets. Don't tell me you forgot our big celebration night — being treated to dinner *and* a basketball game by my wonderful dad?"

Collette slumped back in her seat, her cheeks flaming. "I remember you saying *some*thing about that a couple of weeks ago, but . . ."

"I said the first home game they play the Celts, which is Friday."

"Well, I didn't realize it was this Friday," stammered Collette. "I mean, I was invited to Sherri's slumber party and I already said I would definitely be there."

"What?" Marsha scowled at Collette. "I mentioned this game *way* before you started hanging around with all those show-off eighth-graders. Boy, wait till I call Sarah."

Collette shook her head. "You mentioned something but then you and Sarah got so mad at me that I thought it was canceled. That's when I agreed to go to Sherri's sleepover."

"Well, unagree," Marsha said simply. "Tell her my dad went to a lot of trouble to get these expensive tickets and make reservations at a fancy restaurant and . . ." Marsha peered over the top of her book bag at Collette. "Unless you'd really rather forget about your real friends and go hang around with a bunch of strangers all night."

"They aren't strangers, Marsha. They are being really nice to you and Sarah, too."

"Ha!" Marsha spat out the laugh like it had been choking her. "On Tuesday when you left early to go to the dentist, Sarah and I walked over to their table and they didn't even say hello. We felt really dumb. Luckily I pretended I just needed more napkins and we kept walking."

Collette felt terrible. It was getting harder and harder to keep Marsha and Sarah happy and still spend time with Sherri and her great friends. Why did it all have to be so confusing when it should be so easy for everyone to like each other?

"Wait till I tell Sarah," repeated Marsha. "She won't believe this at all." Marsha stared out the window and shook her head.

Collette sighed. "What am I supposed to say to Sherri?"

"Tell her the *truth*, Collette. Tell her that you already made plans with your two best friends. Tell her to leave you alone." Marsha put her hand on Collette's shoulder. "Please . . . I've been looking forward to Friday. Working so closely with Roger is driving me crazy! Now my parents are talking about how great it would be if Roger and I win at Hershey and get to go to Washington.

131

My mother is going to call Roger's mom and suggest we all go out for lunch afterwards." Marsha groaned. "If anyone sees me with him in public, I'll move away."

The bus stopped and the girls walked off without speaking. "Marsha, I'll call you later." Maybe later she would know what to do.

"Call Sherri and tell her you can't come," pleaded Marsha. "Do it for me. Roger is coming over tonight to help paint stalactites, so I need something nice to look forward to."

"I'll talk to you later about it. Bye." Collette clutched her book bag and raced across the street. Marsha was right. Collette had been dumb to tell Sherri she would go to her party when Marsha had already invited her to the game. But after the fight, it didn't seem like Marsha would be talking to Collette for a long, long time. Collette sighed. She felt so guilty and confused.

"Boy, you sure look thoughtful." Her mother took Collette's book bag and held open the side door. "I hope you and Marsha aren't fighting again."

Collette shook her head. "Yes — I mean, no. Sherri wants me to spend the night at her house on Friday and Marsha wants me to go to the Celts game Friday night."

"Who asked you first?"

The question sounded so simple, but it wasn't. "Marsha, but then she got real mad at me and I thought I was uninvited. So I told Sherri I would go to her house." Collette paused, almost wishing her mom would tell her what to do like she used to.

"You better make a decision soon, Collette. You're going to have to disappoint someone."

The phone rang before Collette could ask her mom to decide which girl to disappoint.

"Collette, it's for you!" Jeff shouted down the stairs. "Hurry up and get off so I can call Keto."

Collette walked into the kitchen and grabbed the phone. "Hello?"

"Hi." It was Sherri. Collette wrapped the phone cord around and around her hand. Now would be the perfect time to explain everything to Sherri. She wouldn't be able to go to her party after all. There would be lots of other girls there. No one would miss her that much.

"Listen, Collette," said Sherri. "I have a real big favor to ask. Just say no if you don't want to, but

I was wondering if you could get that team picture with your dad and Mr. Kurtlander and bring it to the party on Friday. The girls will just die when they see it."

Collette's heart tripped a beat. She should just open her mouth and start explaining right now and get it over with.

"My mom just got home. She bought five bags of junk for the party," Sherri continued. "She even bought marshmallows and chocolate squares so we can make s'mores."

Collette could hear Sherri's mother saying something in the background, but Sherri covered up the phone.

"So anyway . . ." Sherri started to laugh. "No, Mom, don't."

"Hello, Collette?"

Collette stood up straighter. Was this Sherri's mom?

"Hi, Mrs. Anders."

Collette could hear more laughter. "Collette, Sherri doesn't want anyone to know but it is her birthday and I think it would be fun if you all brought a baby picture to the party and then tried to guess each other's identity."

Collette could hear Sherri in the background. "*Mother!* That is *so* queer."

Mrs. Anders laughed again. "Well, it was just an idea. Tell the others if you get a chance."

"My mom is so excited about my birthday," giggled Sherri when she got back on the line.

Another rush of guilt washed over Collette. Now how was she supposed to tell Sherri she couldn't come?

"So anyway, I'll see you in school tomorrow, okay?"

"Sure," said Collette. "Bye."

"Don't forget the picture," Sherri reminded before she hung up. "You'll be the hit of the party."

Collette stood holding the phone until the dial tone disappeared and a recording told her to please hang up. She did what it said, relieved that somebody was finally telling her what to do.

Chapter Fifteen

Mrs. Cessano insisted on driving Collette and Marsha to school on Friday morning. Collette looked down at her science project, then tightened the wire leading to the light bulb. She had finished painting the title, *Electricity: The Marvel of Electrolytes!*, late last night. She bit her lip and tried not to frown. Actually, the lettering had taken the longest to do. Collette usually spent hours and hours on projects. Not this time. She sighed. Lately she was spending more and more time just trying to stay friendly with Sarah, Marsha, and Sherri. Keeping friends friendly got a lot harder in the sixth grade.

136

"Thanks for driving me to school, Mrs. Cessano," Collette said.

Mrs. Cessano turned and flashed Collette a happy smile. She waved her hand and then patted Marsha's shoulder so hard her gold bracelets clattered and chimed like a tambourine.

"Happy to do it, dear. I couldn't have you two scientists trying to drag these masterpieces on the bus. Marsha and that cute Roger spent another two hours on it last night, just adding the finishing touches."

Marsha turned and rolled her eyes at Collette. "Roger is so weird."

Mrs. Cessano laughed as she turned into the school's drive. "Methinks you do protest too much, Marsha."

Marsha groaned. "Methinks Roger is still a creep, Mom."

As soon as the car stopped, Collette grinned and climbed out. Mrs. Cessano pushed open her door and flew around to help Marsha.

"Do you want me to help carry it in, Marsha?" Mrs. Cessano held onto her daughter's elbow as she helped her move slowly across the playground.

"No, thanks. Mom, stop acting like I'm carrying your first grandchild or something. It's just a science experiment."

Mrs. Cessano winked at Collette. "Just a science experiment! I think it's good enough to win first place, don't you, Collette?" Mrs. Cessano stretched her hand out toward Collette. "Oh, excuse me, Collette. Yours is just . . . just wonderful, too. I'm sure you girls will both win."

Collette stared down at her light bulb and generator. Except for the fancy lettering, it looked pretty boring compared to Marsha's elaborate cave with stalactites and stalagmites growing everywhere. Marsha and Roger had even added trees and a tiny toothpick bridge. It looked wonderful!

"Well, I guess I better get going." Mrs. Cessano shot Marsha another worried look. "Are you sure you can manage?"

"Hey . . . don't move another step!"

Collette watched Roger charge across the playground, his camera swinging wildly from a strap around his neck. "Wait, I need a picture . . . 'Science Experiment Finally Unveiled.' " He laughed hard and started clicking pictures.

"Will you stop that!" shouted Marsha. "Get a life, Roger!"

Roger was walking backward, nodding. "Looks good. I couldn't get any TV coverage of this auspicious event, but these pictures will tell the whole story." Roger snapped the lens cover on. "Okay, you can take the next picture of me as I slide this baby onto the display table in the all-purpose room."

Collette laughed. "Are a lot of projects already inside, Roger?"

Roger took the project from Marsha and walked toward the door. "About fifty, at least. You should see some of them."

Marsha looked worried. "Better than ours?"

Roger winked back at her. "Don't worry, Sugar-Lips, our project puts them all to shame."

Marsha shuddered and yanked open the door. "If you call me Sugar-Lips, Honey Bear, or Pretty Woman one more time, Roger Friday, I am going to rip off one of those stalactites and chase you off this planet."

Roger breezed past, winking at Marsha again. "You're gorgeous when you're angry, Funny Face."

Marsha screamed so loudly, Collette almost dropped her project. Roger grinned and hurried into the school.

"Marsha, calm down," warned Collette. "If Mr. Kurtlander sees you fighting with Roger, he'll make you two work on another project together."

Marsha shivered. "Please — I've suffered enough. I am so glad it's finally over. Roger is out of my life again."

"Hey, there's Sarah," Collette said, hurrying up the stairs and into the school. "Sarah, over here!"

Sarah turned and waved. "Marsha, I just saw your project. It looks great. Collette, yours looks wonderful, too. Wait till you see mine. My yeast looks so sick."

"Do you really like mine?" asked Marsha. "Did you notice the tiny deer drinking from the stream outside the cave? Roger made that out of clay and painted it. It looks so real, it's incredible. I never knew he was so good in art."

"You and Roger even put a bird nest in the tree," added Sarah. "You guys are going to win for sure."

Marsha smiled. "Thanks. We sure spent enough time on it."

Collette giggled. "Well, if you win, you will be spending even *more* time with Roger. The car ride to Hershey is over four hours, Marsha."

Marsha's eyes bugged out. "But, I don't have

to go *with* Roger. I mean, my parents and I can go, and then . . ."

Sarah nudged Collette. "Yes, but parents love to organize these events. If you win, they will decide how convenient it would be if all six of you drove up together."

"Kind of like being on tour," laughed Collette.

Marsha leaned against the lockers, slapping her forehead with her hand. "What if we win and go on to Washington, D.C.? And what if we win there? I bet we'll be on the morning news and then the whole world will hear Roger — " Marsha swallowed hard — "call me Sugar-Lips — in front of a trillion people, too, and . . ."

Collette and Sarah started to laugh.

Marsha shot back to attention. "It's not funny, not a bit of it. Just because I did a great science experiment, doesn't mean I have to spend the *rest of my life* with Roger Friday! There's got to be a way out of this mess, and I'm going to find it."

Marsha stormed down the hall, her arms swinging back and forth like a general walking into the front line.

"Whoa . . . what set her off?"

Collette turned and smiled at Sherri and Angela. "She doesn't want to win first place anymore," explained Collette.

Sherri nodded. "Roger showed me their project. It really is fantastic. It's one of the best."

Collette shifted her own in her arms. "They worked three times harder on theirs than I did. At least my light bulb lights up."

"You should see Sherri's," said Angela. "It is the best one in there."

"Angela..." Sherri shook back her hair, looking embarrassed.

"It *is*. She has all these great charts and real bean plants." Angela patted Sherri on the back. "You'll end up in Washington, D.C."

"I hope so." Sherri looked sad all of a sudden. "My dad promised me he would take me if I won. No matter what."

"That would be great, Sherri," said Collette. She knew how much Sherri missed being with her dad.

The morning bell rang and the girls all groaned.

"Bye, Collette and Sarah," Sherri called as she grabbed Angela's arm and hurried up the stairs. "See you at lunch. I'll save you a seat at our table."

Sarah took hold of Collette's arm. "Maybe you

better eat with Sherri and I'll eat with Marsha. She was pretty upset this morning."

Collette slid her project down on table eighteen and smiled at Sarah. "I'll eat with you and Marsha. I'll explain about it to Sherri." She linked arms with Sarah as they hurried out the door. "Nobody can split up the Three Musketeers. It's *scientifically* impossible!"

Chapter Sixteen

"You're splitting us up, Collette! All because of Sherri Anders!"

The three girls sat in the cafeteria, staring at the floor, out the window, anywhere but at each other.

"I feel terrible," Collette said softly.

"*You* feel terrible." Marsha leaned across the table and scowled at Collette. "Think of my dad. My poor dad already bought your ticket and made reservations for dinner. I bet you're not the least bit sorry, either."

"Marsha!" Sarah scooted closer to Collette on the cafeteria bench. "Collette just said she was sorry she couldn't go with us. How many times does she have to say it?"

Marsha just shrugged like maybe a million times would be nice. "I know that going to a basketball game with my dad is not as glamorous as going to Sherri Anders's private birthday celebration. But you did tell us yesterday that you were going to try and think of a nice way to get out of going to her party," reminded Marsha.

"I know, and I was up all last night thinking and thinking." Collette took a long drink of milk, wishing she knew what to say to convince Sarah and Marsha that they were just as important as Sherri. "But Sherri called me at nine-thirty last night to — "

Marsha whacked down her sandwich. "Nine-thirty! Your mother never lets me call past eight o'clock at your house."

Collette sighed. "Believe me she wasn't thrilled that Sherri called that late. The phone woke up Stevie and . . ." Collette took a deep breath. "Anyway, Sherri was real upset because her dad won't be able to come for her birthday after all. He won't be able to come to Pittsburgh for another two weeks."

145

"That's too bad," Sarah said.

"So I couldn't say, 'Well, Sherri, while we're on the subject, *I* can't come to your party either.'" Collette was glad to see Sarah nodding. Sarah knew how special birthdays were.

"Sherri sounded like she was going to cry," Collette added. "She said she wished she could just cancel the whole party."

Marsha craned her neck toward the noisy eighth-grade section of the cafeteria. "Well, she seems to have recovered now. She's surrounded by her love slaves!"

Collette and Sarah twisted around. Sherri was standing up, laughing and shoving Ricky and his friends toward the door. Ricky kept putting his hands together like he was praying, but Sherri kept shaking her head and laughing harder.

"That Ricky is so weird," muttered Marsha. "He acts like Sherri is some sort of goddess. I heard he gave her a solid gold bracelet yesterday. At lunchtime his mother came to school to get it back 'cause he had taken it from her jewelry box."

"No!" Collette and Sarah looked at each other, horrified. Stealing from your own mother for the girl you loved!

"And . . ." Marsha waited till both girls were

absolutely quiet. "Roger told me Ricky wrote, 'I love Sherri Anders' on the wall in the boys' room. He even put his initials."

"The janitor will be able to trace him," Collette whispered. All three girls turned and stared again at someone so much in love he would risk getting kicked out of school by Sister Mary Elizabeth.

"Boy, is he dumb," whispered Collette.

Marsha stood up, shoving both hands on her hips and sighing. "Lots of people are acting dumb because of Sherri Anders."

Collette's cheeks started blazing. She stared down at her cheese crackers, flicking them back and forth between her fingers. Why couldn't Marsha just let things drop? Why couldn't she try to understand like Sarah?

"I have a great idea," said Sarah brightly. She leaned over and popped one of Collette's cheese crackers in her mouth and grinned. "Call us as soon as you get home from Sherri's tomorrow, Collette. We can go to a movie."

Collette looked up. Sarah smiled again. "My mom can drop us off at Cheswick."

"Mine can pick us up," offered Collette. She looked up at Marsha. "What movie would you like to see, Marsha? You can pick."

Marsha flung her dark hair back like a cape, still frowning. "I don't know. My dad might be so mad about that unused basketball ticket, he might just ground me and . . ."

Sarah and Collette started to laugh. Marsha looked down and gave a lopsided grin. "I'll check the papers. Listen, I better go upstairs and call my mom. She can give the ticket away." Marsha made a face. "I hope she doesn't suggest Roger come with us."

Sarah groaned. "No, thank you."

"Mr. Kurtlander thinks you and Roger did a great job," said Collette. "He practically gave you both a standing ovation when he saw your project."

Marsha's cheeks flushed pink. "I know. He said we both have an automatic A for the semester. Unless we do something awful, like fail a test." Marsha looked up at the clock. "I'll meet you guys outside in a couple of minutes."

Sarah and Collette threw away their trash and hurried outside. The sun was melting the last bit of snow.

"Collette, wait up!"

Sherri Anders came running across the playground. Seeing Sherri sent a sudden wave of excitement about the party over Collette. Part of her still couldn't believe she had been invited. Too bad Sherri hadn't invited Marsha and Sarah, too.

"I saw Ricky giving you a hard time in the cafeteria." Collette wanted to steer the conversation away from the party so Sarah wouldn't get upset.

"Oh, that kid drives me crazy." Sherri bumped her shoulder into Collette's. "Speaking of *crazy*, here comes your friend."

Collette and Sarah looked up, then exchanged frightened looks. Marsha was racing across the playground, tears streaming down her cheeks. By the time she reached Collette and Sarah she was crying so hard Collette couldn't understand what she was trying to say.

Roger and his friends stopped playing and charged over. "What's wrong with Marsha?" asked Roger.

Collette put her hand on Marsha's arm. "Marsha, calm down and tell us what happened. Did you get in trouble?"

Marsha shook her head, then drew in a deep breath. When she looked at Roger, she started crying all over again.

"Our science project is . . . is ruined," she sobbed. "It's in a thousand pieces all over the floor!"

Chapter Seventeen

Half the playground fell into step behind Marsha as Collette and Sarah each took an arm and led her back into the building. Roger shoved both hands into his pockets and frowned miserably.

"Is it totally smashed, Marsha?" he asked. "Or just severely dented in certain areas?"

Marsha's mouth wiggled and her eyes glistened. "Trust me, Roger. It looks like someone dropped it off the top of the Empire State Building."

Roger bit his lip. "That bad?"

By the time the group had moved down the hall and into the all-purpose room, Sister Mary Elizabeth and several teachers had hurried out of the teachers' room.

"Children, what is going on?" Sister demanded. "You're not to be inside until the bell rings."

"Somebody smashed our science project!" announced Roger.

Mr. Kurtlander walked quickly out of the teachers' room. "What happened?"

Before anyone could even answer, Mr. Kurtlander crossed the hall and strode into the all-purpose room. Collette cringed when she heard him groan and pound his fist on top of the table.

Marsha gripped Collette's hand more tightly and rushed into the room.

"What on earth happened?" Mr. Kurtlander bent down and picked up two large pieces of the science project.

Roger pushed Marsha forward. "Marsha walked in and found it like this, Mr. Kurtlander. That's why she's so upset."

Mr. Kurtlander turned around. "You found it? When?"

Marsha wiped her cheek with the bottom of her sweater and nodded. "I came up here after lunch and I saw our project scattered all over the floor like a smashed egg."

Mr. Kurtlander frowned. "What were you doing up here in the first place? You were supposed to be outside."

Collette jumped at the angry sound in Mr. Kurtlander's voice. Marsha stood up a little straighter, like she had just remembered she was talking to a teacher. An angry teacher.

"Well, I had to call my mother and . . ."

Mr. Kurtlander tossed the large pieces down on the table. "The phone's in the office. I still don't understand how you ended up in the all-purpose room. The doors were closed. There is a big sign stating that no one was allowed in."

Marsha's eyes grew wide. "I thought the sign was for kids who didn't have a project. I mean, I only wanted to look at my project one more time. I couldn't remember if Roger remembered to paste the sign on and . . ." Marsha trailed off. Collette and Sarah exchanged looks. Anyone who knew Marsha could tell that she was getting mad. Marsha shoved her fingers through her bangs and then tugged them back down again.

"Yeah, Marsha and I talked about that," said Roger quickly. "Downstairs, I got to thinking that maybe I forgot to add that sign and I'm glad she came up here to check."

Mr. Kurtlander didn't even look over at Roger. He was still staring a hole right through Marsha.

"So you came in here and the project was already all over the floor?" asked Mr. Kurtlander. "You didn't touch a thing?"

Marsha nodded. "*I* didn't do it, Mr. Kurtlander. Why would I break my own project?"

Sister Mary Elizabeth put her arm around Marsha's shoulder. "Mr. Kurtlander wasn't accusing you, Marsha. This is a terrible tragedy. We are trying to figure out the facts, that's all." Sister looked up as more students pushed into the room. "Go back outside, all of you. I don't want to see you again until the bell rings."

Collette and Sarah took a step closer to Marsha. Collette reached out and squeezed Marsha's hand.

Sister clapped her hands and herded the children out. She stood at the doorway and looked back at Collette and Sarah. "Girls, Roger, I think Mr. Kurtlander would like to talk to Marsha alone for a few minutes to gather some facts."

"I better stay," added Roger. "The project was half mine."

Marsha reached out and grabbed onto Collette's

arm. She shot Mr. Kurtlander a disappointed look. "Wait, can't Collette and Sarah stay? I was with them the whole time at lunch and . . . Mr. Kurtlander, I didn't break this project. Why would I? I didn't . . ." Marsha opened her mouth and started crying. She just stood there and cried like her whole heart was smashed to bits, too.

Mr. Kurtlander looked at her carefully.

Roger shifted from foot to foot. "Yeah, I mean . . . well, don't cry, Marsha. I know you didn't do it. I mean . . ." Roger reached out and patted Marsha awkwardly on the back. "You may have your bad days, Marsha, but at least you're always up front about them." Roger scratched his chin. "I mean . . . you aren't the sneaky type to stab people in the back. If you want to stab someone, you do it right out in the open which is, well, kind of honest."

Mr. Kurtlander and Sister Mary Elizabeth started laughing. Finally Collette and Sarah smiled and even Marsha looked up and rolled her eyes at Roger.

"Thanks, Roger," Marsha said, wiping her tears. She gave a short laugh. "I think."

Mr. Kurtlander grinned at Marsha. "I believe you," he said.

"If someone accidently bumped into the table, then I could understand this," he said slowly. "But that wouldn't explain the utter destruction. I think someone deliberately destroyed this project." He rubbed his hand over his face. "But why? That's what I can't understand."

Collette shook her head. Whoever did this had to have planned it. Planned meanness was scary.

Mr. Kurtlander moved a few pieces of the plaster cave with the tip of his loafer. "I sure am sorry that the judges in Hershey never got a chance to see this project. You guys had a real chance at the blue ribbon with this."

Marsha sighed and let Sarah give her a hug. Collette knew Marsha's heart must be totally broken. Marsha was not a real hugger.

Roger bent down and picked up the tiny brown deer. Except for a chipped ear, it looked fine. He handed it to Marsha. "Here. I can fix that ear in a minute. In fact, I think we can fix a lot of this."

Marsha blinked. "You're nuts. This project is ruined, finished, out for the count."

Roger grinned. "No way. I don't get mad, Marsha. I get even." Sister Mary Elizabeth's eyebrows shot up.

Roger bent down and gathered a handful of

large pieces, "Look, Marsha. The trees are okay, the stalactites still look like long teeth. We can still use them. How hard can it be to fix the whole mess?"

"Real hard," insisted Marsha. "It took me two hours just to do that bridge."

"I'll help," offered Roger. "That will knock it down to one hour."

Marsha sighed. She pulled on her bangs. "We'll never make it in time for the contest."

Marsha looked up at Mr. Kurtlander. "You're picking the finalists today, aren't you?"

Mr. Kurtlander looked around the room, shoving both hands into his pockets. "Well, I don't know. I thought we would pick the finalists today, but that was before I realized how many projects were entered. It may take me until . . . until Monday to come up with the winning four. . . ." Mr. Kurtlander reached over and tugged Marsha's ponytail. "Maybe Monday afternoon. Would that give you two enough time?"

Collette smiled, hugging herself as the goose bumps raced up her arms. Monday afternoon was a whole weekend away. Two whole days. Anything could happen before then.

Chapter Eighteen

"If we start tonight, we'll be able to get it finished," announced Marsha.

On the bus ride home from school, Marsha seemed energized, ready to reglue and rebuild the science project. "Whoever thought they could run Marsha Cessano out of town is in for a rude awakening," she added.

"You have so much work to do!" pointed out Collette.

"Roger is coming over at six-thirty," explained Marsha. She licked the tip of her pencil and checked off two lines. "Sarah is coming at six, right after her ballet lesson. We'll get started by seven."

"What about the basketball game and dinner?" Collette leaned forward and tried to read what Marsha had been scribbling in her notebook all afternoon.

Marsha snapped shut the notebook and sighed like a tired businessman. "Well, plans change, Collette. While you were washing the boards, Roger, Sarah, and I decided that we've got to catch the enemy by surprise. We've got to have a brand-new, improved project back on the table by Monday morning. My dad will be behind us, one-hundred percent. In fact, I bet my Uncle Norman, a real security guard, may want to drop by the school on Monday to ask a few questions."

Collette nodded, proud that Marsha was willing to fight back this way. She just wished that they would wait until Saturday afternoon to launch their attack, so she could help.

"Roger called his mom and she called my mom." Marsha smiled shyly. "Roger said I was too upset to discuss the facts. He said he would handle it."

"Does Mr. Kurtlander have any idea who ruined your project?"

Marsha shook her head. "He didn't say. Face

it — our project was so good, it made some kid spaz out. Some poor kid who spent the last few weeks growing root rot in his basement just looked at our project and realized he didn't have a chance." Marsha sighed as she stared out the window.

"I wish I could help," Collette said. "Maybe I could come over tomorrow . . ."

Marsha shook her head. "We'll be finished by then, Collette. My mom will probably let us drink coffee and everything tonight, just to stay awake. This is one of those emergency type things where all normal rules fly right out the window."

Collette gripped her book bag, feeling left out already. It was only the knowledge that she would be having lots of fun at Sherri's slumber party that kept her from begging Marsha to please let her come and help glue back the cave.

Collette wished Marsha good luck and raced up her driveway. She still had so much to do. Wash her hair, pack her overnight bag. She still wasn't sure if she should bring pajamas or just sleep in a huge football jersey like they did in the movies.

Football! Collette took the steps two at a time and went into her dad's bedroom. He had left his football team picture propped up against his alarm clock for Collette to take to the party.

Collette took the picture and wrapped it carefully in blue tissue. Her dad trusted her with his only copy and she didn't want to injure it.

Collette packed in a hurry and then stared at the clock until it was time to leave. She was so excited she didn't even mind when Laura and Stevie insisted on riding along with them.

"Do you get to eat popcorn all night?" asked Stevie. "And never go to sleep?"

"If we want," laughed Collette. She saw her mother frown and then shook her hand. "But I'll go to bed early so I won't be in a grumpy mood tomorrow."

Collette's mother smiled. "Thanks, honey. I'll be by around nine-thirty then."

As soon as the car stopped, Collette picked up her duffle bag. "Bye." Collette leaned over and kissed her mom, then turned and waved to Stevie and Laura. "Bye, guys. If I get any candy treats, I'll save them for you."

"Bye, Collette." Both Stevie and Laura leaned over the seat and hugged part of her. Collette patted them, trying to break away. She would die

160

if she looked up and saw the eighth-grade girls watching from the windows.

Collette stood on the front porch, ringing the bell and waving as her mother's car drove slowly down the road. She hoped Sherri would answer soon, before her mother decided to back up and wait.

"Hi, Collette!" Sherri opened the door and pulled Collette inside. "We've been waiting for you!"

"Happy birthday, Sherri," Collette said.

"Thank you!" cried Sherri. She grinned and hugged Collette. "Come on up. We're giving each other facials and manicures."

Collette followed Sherri up the stairs, smiling at the happy sounds coming from the apartment. She could smell the popcorn, and the music sounded great.

The apartment looked so festive. A big *Happy Birthday* banner hung over the sink, and red-and-white helium balloons were tied to the backs of the kitchen chairs.

"Here she is guys," announced Sherri. She pulled Collette right into the room like she really was the guest everyone had been waiting for.

"Hi, Collette," said a lot of the girls right away.

Collette nodded and smiled at everyone. Most of the girls she already recognized, but there were some strange faces mixed in.

"Who is she?" asked a tall girl with blonde wavy hair.

"I think she's related to Mr. Kurtlander or something," replied the shorter girl. "I think she's his niece or something."

Collette dropped her tote bag and reached for a handful of popcorn. She suddenly felt like she was the new girl way back in kindergarten again.

"What are we supposed to do with the baby pictures?" asked Angela. "Mine is so gross. Why did my mother make me wear a bonnet in every single picture?"

"Because you were bald, Angela," laughed another girl.

"Oh, my gosh," said Collette. "I completely forgot about bringing my baby picture."

Sherri just laughed and handed Collette a can of soda. "Oh, don't worry about it. Almost everyone forgot." Sherri drummed her long pink nails on the counter. "The important question is, did you remember Mr. Kurtlander's football picture?"

At the mention of his name, several girls started screaming like a rock star had just walked into the kitchen.

"Let me see," cried Kathy, grabbing a tissue and wiping the green goop from her face.

Collette reached in her pocket. "Be careful because my dad wants it back and . . ."

Before Collette could even finish, the picture was being passed around like a new baby.

"Oh, is he cute!"

"Look at the shoulders on him," gushed Angela. "What a hunk!"

"I can't believe how young he looks," laughed another. "Hey, which one is your dad, Collette?"

Collette was proud to squirm her way into the center and point out her dad.

"Collette, you should get about a hundred reprints made of this, and make a fortune at lunch selling them," suggested Sherri. She took the picture and kissed it, then flipped it over. "Hey, what's this? Carrie at 555-8729."

"Ooooh, a phone number!" cried the girls.

Collette's heart flipped. She had forgotten all about Mr. Kurtlander writing the number down for her mother. She should have erased it.

"Who is Carrie?" asked Sherri. "Miss Mystery Lady?"

Collette tried to keep a smile on her face. Everyone in the whole kitchen was staring at her like she was in the witness box. "I don't know."

Sherri studied Collette for a second and then grinned. She held the picture high in the air and marched into the living room. "Okay, girls, time to start some games."

"Shouldn't your mom be back with the pizza?" asked Angela. "I'm starving!"

Sherri sat on the braided rug and held up the picture. "Time for Truth or Dare!"

A few of the girls groaned, but most of them started to clap and whistle. Collette followed the others into the living room. She had never played this slumber party game before. Wait until she told Marsha and Sarah! She hoped it didn't mean you had to try a puff of a cigarette or chug a whole can of ginger ale in one gulp.

As soon as the girls were seated in a circle, Sherri leaned forward. "Okay now, Angela will be first."

Angela covered her eyes. "Why do I always have to be first?"

Sherri laughed. "Cause you're my good friend. Okay now, Angela, truth or dare. Did you cheat on your diet after school today?"

Angela groaned and covered her face. A couple of girls giggled.

When Angela finally pulled her hands away, her face was bright red. "I don't want to answer. What's my dare?"

Sherri stared up at the ceiling for a second, thinking. "The dare is . . . is to go outside and sit by the stop sign with a container of yogurt on your head." Sherri grinned as everyone started to laugh, even Angela. "You have to wait till at least three cars drive by."

"Can I eat the yogurt?" Angela asked. Angela stood up, then sat down again. "I'd rather tell the truth. Okay, so I cheated. I ate a few cookies, one very small bowl of chips, drank a can of soda, *diet* soda, girls, and . . ."

"And a partridge and a pear tree," sang out a short girl sitting next to Collette.

Collette laughed now, beginning to relax. Truth or dare was fun. Maybe she could play it at her next slumber party with Marsha and Sarah.

Collette felt her cheeks grow warm, thinking

about how hard Marsha must be working right now, trying to fix her science project.

"My turn," Angela said, looking around the room, her finger aimed at each girl. "Okay, Dana, truth or dare. How many times did you kiss Mike Bossola at Lesley's party last Saturday?"

The room exploded with laughter. Dana leaned over and swatted Angela on the shoulder. Angela stood up and raised both hands. "And part two, Dana . . . is Mike a good kisser?"

Dana hopped up from the floor and started chasing Angela around the circle. Collette thought it looked really funny, like an eighth-grade version of Duck-Duck-Goose.

After Dana caught Angela and pretended to strangle her, she grinned and sat back down. "Well, I am going to take the truth, of course, since I have nothing to hide."

Dana tossed her long dark braid over her left shoulder and cleared her throat. "The truth is, girls, that I did *not* kiss Mike Bossola, cute as he is."

"Oh, sure!" hooted Kathy and Angela together.

Dana tugged at her braid. "I mean it. Mike spreads those rumors around himself." She started to laugh. "He's trying to become a legend in his own time."

Everyone started talking at once, passing the popcorn and pretzel dishes around the circle.

Sherri glanced at her watch. "Okay, guys, time for one more before my mom gets here with the pizza."

Collette looked around the circle, hoping Mary Lee or Margie would be called on next. They were both so pretty and funny.

Collette snapped a pretzel and grinned. Eighth-grade parties were fun.

"Truth or dare," began Sherri. She pointed her own pretzel across the circle. "For our very special guest tonight — Collette!"

Chapter Nineteen

The whole room got quiet. Angela set the pop-corn down and dusted off her fingers. Everyone leaned closer like Collette was about to give a speech.

"Sure," said Collette. The girls were probably a little more interested in her turn since she was new, the biggest stranger in the group.

"Truth or dare, Collette, tell us everything you know about this mysterious Carrie person mentioned on the back of Mr. Kurtlander's picture."

Collette felt a thousand prickles racing across her back like she had just been tossed onto a bed of nails.

"Yeah, who is she?" asked Dana. "Does he have a girlfriend?"

"Does he want one?" giggled Mary Lee. "I'm available!"

Sherri passed the picture across to Collette. "Who is she? Remember, you're honor bound to tell the truth."

Collette stared down at the picture and frowned. The truth was, Carrie was Mr. Kurtlander's business and nobody else's.

Collette tapped her finger against the picture. "I've never met this Carrie. I guess she's somebody from his past."

Sherri laughed. "Of course, Collette, that's why we want to know about her. Come on, your parents must have mentioned something about her when they loaned you this picture."

Collette traced her fingers along the braided rug. She tried to keep her voice light and carefree. "Well, it's private stuff. My parents would get really mad if I talked about it."

A few girls groaned. Collette saw Kathy lean over and overheard her whisper to Mary Lee. "Of course it's private. Holy cow, why does she think she was invited anyway?"

Sherri pointed her pretzel at Collette again. "Okay, you know the rules, Collette. If you don't tell the truth, you have to do the dare."

Collette sat up straighter, relieved. She would much rather sit outside with a bowl of popcorn on her head than announce a lot of private, personal facts about Mr. Kurtlander.

Sherri leaned forward. "Your dare — " Sherri smiled at everyone in the circle — "is to call the number on the back of the picture and ask for Carrie. We can ask her some questions."

"Great idea!" A lot of the girls started clapping. A few patted Sherri on the back for masterminding such a terrific dare.

Collette picked up the picture and stared at it. Mr. Kurtlander squinted back against the sun-filled football field. "But my dare is almost the same as my truth."

Sherri shrugged. "That's how the game is played in the eighth grade, Collette."

Collette bit her lip. "I can't call . . ."

Angela shook her head. "Honestly!"

"This Carrie must be someone important," laughed Kathy. "Maybe Mr. Kurtlander left her at the altar or something."

"Or maybe Mr. Kurtlander is still in love with her but she dumped him and he is walking around with a broken heart," suggested another girl.

"Are you nuts?" laughed Sherri. "Nobody would dump someone as cute as Mr. Kurtlander. I bet the only reason half the girls in the school entered that science contest was to get a chance to spend more time with him in Hershey."

"He is so handsome," sighed Dana. "A *real* legend."

"I'll tell you all about it when I get back from Hershey," Sherri said smugly. "And I'll send you all a postcard from Washington, D.C."

Everyone started talking about the trip and how cute Mr. Kurtlander was. Collette sighed, glad that she was off the hook.

"Come on, Collette, time to call," shouted Angela.

Collette shook her head. "Ask me to do something else, please?"

"Honestly Collette," Sherri said impatiently. She took the picture from Collette. "How hard can it be to call this number and ask for Carrie? You don't have to tell them who you are. Pretend you're from a marketing company. Ask her what kind of tuna fish she buys, which toothpaste she uses, and then ask her if she still loves our Mr. Kurtlander."

A lot of the girls started to stand up. Mary Lee and Margie pulled Collette to her feet. "Come on, Collette. It will be fun."

Collette tried to smile, but inside her heart was beating a mile a minute. She let herself be dragged to the phone, but she shook her head and put her hands behind her back when Sherri tried to hand her the receiver.

"Wait. Carrie is just someone from Mr. Kurtlander's past and . . . it's *his* life. I can't just . . ." Collette tried to swallow, but her mouth was too dry. "I can't butt into his life that way. It isn't fair."

"Oh, brother," muttered someone near the sink. "Sermon time!"

"Where did Sherri find her?" whispered another girl. "The convent?"

Sherri shook back her hair and laughed. "Calm down. Wait a minute now, girls. I'll show Collette how easy it is. I'll call someone and pretend to be Miss Mary Marketing." Sherri grinned at Collette. "It isn't a big deal."

172

Collette smiled back, glad to see the other girls nodding and laughing again.

"Okay now, who should I call?" asked Sherri.

"Ricky!" called out Kathy.

Sherri made a face. "Oh, please!"

Angela moved closer and punched out some numbers. "You promised him you would call him for the next seven days, to thank him for helping you with the science competition, remember?"

"Yeah, Mr. Love Slave really took a chance for you, Sherri," added Dana. "I still can't believe he did it."

Sherri's face flooded red. "Drop it."

Angela nudged Sherri. "It's ringing. Old Ricky boy will be thrilled! Thank your biggest fan for sneaking — "

"Shut up, Angela," snapped Sherri. The room got quiet quickly. Sherri glared at the girls. "Talk about having a big mouth."

Angela looked miserable. "Well, what's the big deal, Sherri? No one's blaming you for what Ricky did!"

Sherri slammed the phone down. "Be quiet."

Angela looked around the room, her frown beginning as soon as she saw Collette. "Oh . . ."

Collette glanced up at Sherri. Should she tell her that she already knew about Ricky giving her the stolen gold bracelet, and how he wrote on the wall in the boys' room?

"Hey, I already know about Ricky," said Collette. She saw the stricken look on Sherri's face. "It isn't your fault Sherri. I mean, this guy must have a huge crush on you and that's why he did that crazy stuff."

Sherri broke into a huge grin. She looked relieved as she smiled at Collette. "Exactly, and I would have stopped him if I had known."

Angela winked. "Yeah, but now that Marsha's project is out of the competition, you're a whole lot closer to Hershey, Sherri."

The room got noisy with talking and laughter again. Collette stepped forward. "What? What did Ricky do?"

Before Sherri even opened her mouth, Collette knew the answer. "Ricky smashed Roger and Marsha's project, didn't he?" Collette looked at Sherri. "I can't believe he did something so terrible."

Sherri shrugged. "You said you knew about it. Anyway, I didn't *ask* him to do it, Collette."

Angela nodded. "Yeah, Ricky follows Sherri around all the time. He knew Sherri wanted to win so he just kind of helped out." Angela giggled. "I'm afraid Ricky is more muscle than brain."

"Ricky said he wanted to knock two seventh-grade projects off the table, too, but he heard someone coming," Kathy said, "He hid in the storage closet for five minutes!"

"Marsha and Roger worked for weeks on that project," Collette said quietly.

"You aren't going to turn him in, are you?" asked Sherri. "Collette, you would be getting the whole eighth-grade class in trouble if you did."

"There goes our graduation dance," groaned somebody.

"Sister Mary Elizabeth will probably cancel Kennywood amusement park, too," added Mary Lee. "She'll probably make us all go to confession and say nine hundred Hail Marys."

"I'm not going to tell Sister or Mr. Kurtlander," said Collette. "But I think it stinks."

Angela raised an eyebrow and started to laugh. "Well, excuse me."

Sherri reached out and patted Collette on the shoulder. "Hey, don't get so upset. Marsha and

175

Roger are only in the sixth grade. They can do another great project next year."

Angela held out the phone. "Let's get busy with those calls, girls."

Collette picked up the football picture from the kitchen table. She looked at Mr. Kurtlander and her dad and then flipped it over and stared at Carrie's number.

"Way to go, Collette," two girls cheered from the counter. "Let's get the party rolling."

As she reached for the phone, Collette was glad her hand wasn't shaking. She wasn't as nervous as she thought she was going to be.

"If Mr. Kurtlander answers, I will die," Sherri whispered, leaning her head close to Collette's.

"Hello, Mom?"

"Mom?" groaned several girls.

"Give me a break," Kathy muttered, crossing her arms. "Ricky does something stupid and now we're all a bunch of bad guys."

"Can you pick me up now? . . . Thanks, I'll be watching from the porch." Collette hung up the phone and slid the picture into her back pocket. "I'm going to go home," she said simply. She picked up her duffle bag and hoisted it up on her shoulder. "See you guys later."

Sherri followed Collette down the stairs. At the bottom she sighed. "I wish you wouldn't go, Collette. The girls won't tease you about Carrie anymore. They're really nice."

Collette nodded, glancing up the stairs. Everyone was already laughing about something else.

"I know. Thanks for asking me, Sherri. Happy birthday."

Sherri grinned. "Yeah, fourteen years old!"

Collette turned and opened the door. "I'll just wait outside for my mom. You better go back upstairs with the others."

"Well," Sherri crossed her arms and sighed again. "Are you sure you don't want to change your mind?"

Collette shook her head. "I'm sure." She had been changing her mind back and forth so much lately, it was worn out.

"See you in school," Sherri said cheerfully as she turned and hurried back up the stairs.

Collette shivered as she walked out onto the porch. She zippered her jacket and pulled up her collar. It was still early. She would be home before nine. Enough time to run across the street and help save Roger and Marsha's cave.

Collette gripped her duffel bag and smiled.

Roger was probably driving Marsha crazy right now. Sarah would be busy trying to keep peace and Marsha's mom would be passing fancy treats around as if it were a real party.

Collette grinned, leaning out over the railing to watch for her mother's car, anxious to get to Marsha's as fast as she could.

Chapter Twenty

Roger answered the door. He wiped his floury hands on a checked apron and grinned at Collette.

"Hey, I thought you were hobnobbing with the jet-setters, Collette. I'm glad to see you. Marsha is driving me crazy."

"Collette!" Marsha and Sarah rushed out from the kitchen and hugged her.

"I thought you were at Sherri's party," laughed Sarah. She held up two white hands and made a face. "We are losing the battle with the cave. It looks terrible."

Marsha frowned. "I guess we should just throw it in the trash and give up."

Roger shook his head. "I wish I knew who did

this. I'd drag them over here to help. Then I'd throw them in the trash!"

Collette bit her lip and wondered if she should tell them. By Monday it would be all over school, anyway. Sacred Heart was so small, secrets were impossible to keep.

"Ricky smashed it."

Roger's eyes narrowed. "That creep! No wonder he was asking me lots of questions about our project. How many pages were in our report, what kind of clay we used . . ." Roger took off his apron and tossed it on the bench. "I'm calling Mr. Kurtlander right now."

"Roger," Collette reached out and grabbed his arm. "Listen, I don't want to be the one who blew the whistle. I promised the girls at the party I wouldn't turn Ricky in."

Sarah looked worried. "Why would you promise them anything, Collette? I bet they all knew about it."

Roger made a fist. "Give me two minutes with that kid and . . ."

Marsha handed Roger back his apron. "Put your fist away and put your apron back on. Come on, we've got lots of work to do. My mom should be back any minute with some more clay."

180

"Marsha, I am going to stand up to Ricky, first thing Monday morning," promised Roger. "I'll wait for you so you can watch me defend your honor and our smashed cave."

Marsha turned and crossed her eyes at Roger. "Roger, Ricky is almost six feet tall. He could step on you like a wad of gum. He could toss you on the roof of the school and they wouldn't find you till it was time to clean the gutters. Just stay away from him, okay?"

Roger gave a low bow. "The woman is nuts about me."

Marsha growled. "Getting pulverized by Ricky won't help." Marsha put her hands on her hips. "I would love for Ricky to get in trouble for doing this, but it won't get us back in the contest."

Collette walked into the kitchen, shaking her head at the messy-looking cave. Except for two trees and the repaired deer, it looked terrible. The cave had been glued, but cracks and chips were everywhere.

"I think we have to start over with the cave," said Roger. "This is impossible to repair."

"It will take us all night if we start over." groaned Marsha. She slid into the chair and put her head down. "Look at this cave. It's ruined. No offense, Roger, but it's shaped just like your head."

Roger picked up a dish towel and swatted Marsha. They both grinned.

"Wait a minute," Collette said slowly. "Why don't we just cover up the cracks?"

"We tried, Collette." Sarah held up a tube of brown paint. "This clay keeps on soaking it up and then the cracks show through again. We have about ten coats of paint on it already."

Collette grinned. "Let's go outside and get some real dirt, tiny stones, pieces of evergreen. We can glue it all over the cave. The cracks wouldn't show at all."

"Yeah, it would look real wild and natural," said Roger. "Kind of like when Marsha got that cheap perm back in the third grade."

Marsha grabbed her coat from the brass hook and tossed Roger his jacket. "It amazes me that they ever let you *out* of the third grade, Roger. Didn't you fail coloring, twice?" Everyone laughed, even Roger. Marsha took a small bow. When she stood up, she had a little grin on her face. "I can hardly wait to see the look on Ricky's face when we bring our cave back in Monday. Our project will be even better than before."

Roger nodded. "I'm hiring a guard till the contest."

Collette flicked on Marsha's floodlights and held open the back door. "Sarah, come with me. I want to go to my house and get some more glue. We'll need a lot."

"Wait, don't leave me alone with Roger," laughed Marsha. "I'm sure he's contagious." Marsha turned and waited for him. "At least take your apron off, Roger."

Roger wiggled his eyebrows up and down. "Yes, dear."

As the four of them raced across the street, Collette started to laugh.

"What's so funny?" asked Sarah.

"I was just thinking about this game they were playing at Sherri's party. It's called Truth or Dare. Somebody asks you a question and if you don't want to answer it, you have to do what they dare you to do."

"That sounds fun," said Marsha. "Okay, I go first. Collette, tell us the truth, was it more fun being with a bunch of popular, wild eighth-graders, or is it more fun being with us, the coolest kids in the whole sixth grade?"

Roger grinned. "Well put, Sugar-Lips."

Collette laughed. "Being with you guys, of course."

"Seriously?" asked Sarah. Collette turned and looked at all of them in the glare of the yellow porch light. They were looking right at her like they really needed to know.

"Seriously," Collette said. Then she smiled. "That's the truth, honest."

Roger shivered. "Man, you women really get intense. No wonder you always end up on talk shows. You got to lighten up, smell the roses, go with the flow . . ."

Collette laughed. "Thanks for the advice! You guys hold Roger and I'll run in and get the glue. I think we need to close that mouth of his so we can finally get some work done."

Roger started yelling as he turned and raced down the driveway. "Yeah, you three and who else is going to catch me?"

"After him, women!" ordered Marsha. She grabbed Sarah's hand and they charged across the yard.

Collette let the side door slam and bolted around the house, cornering Roger by the garage. Everyone started laughing as Sarah and Marsha closed in and grabbed Roger by the arms.

184

"I'm innocent, you've got the wrong man!" shouted Roger dramatically. "The only information you'll get from me is my locker number."

Collette grabbed Roger by the scarf, led him back down the driveway, and set him down on the milkbox. "Time for Truth or Dare, Mr. Friday."

Roger hung his head and pretended he was sobbing. "Oh, no, not that! Anything but that!"

Collette stopped in the circle of light by the side door. "Okay, girls, we each get to ask Roger one personal, private question. If he won't answer, we'll glue him to the milkbox all night."

Roger wiggled his eyebrows. "You girls are tough."

"Which science project will get first place in the sixth grade, Roger?" snapped Marsha.

"Ours, of course, dear!"

Sarah bent down and pointed her finger. "Back in the second grade you told everyone you ate three goldfish in one weekend, Roger. Was that true?"

Roger shuddered. "Not *real* goldfish. I was talking about those little fish crackers. Actually, I ate two hundred."

Marsha and Sarah groaned. "You're all talk, Friday."

Finally Collette leaned over and patted Roger on the back. "Now for the toughest one of all, Roger. Remember, you are honor bound to tell the truth."

Roger covered his eyes. "I'm ready."

Collette grinned at Marsha and Sarah, then smiled down at Roger. "Truth or dare, who do you think is the prettiest girl at Sacred Heart?"

Roger's mouth fell open. "Holy cow, that *is* personal, Collette." Roger rose slowly from the milkbox, scratching his head. "But I know I am honor bound to tell the truth, so I'll give you three the answer as soon — " Roger stared up at the sky, then covered his head with his arms. "Wow, look at the comet! It's heading straight for us!"

As the three girls looked up, Roger flew past them laughing as he tore down the driveway. "I'll tell you the truth if you three can catch me!"

"Cheater!" shouted Marsha as she flew down the driveway. "Get back here!"

"You have no honor, Roger Friday!" Sarah yelled. "Catch him, Marsha!"

Collette leaned against the side door, laughing as Roger and Marsha broke through the hedges and flew up the street. Porch lights flashed on as the two raced down the sidewalk, laughing and shouting insults to each other.

"Gosh, look at them, Sarah. They haven't changed a bit since kindergarten!"

"I know. Roger is so funny." Sarah grinned and shook her head. "I can't believe we fell for that comet business."

Collette glanced up into the night. The sky was pitch-black, not a single star or comet in sight. It didn't matter. The happy war cries from Marsha and Roger and being best friends again with Sarah made up for that. It lit up the night more than a million stars ever could.